ACCUSTOMED TO THE DARK

THOMAS DeCONNA

Black Rose Writing | Texas

ISBN: 978-1-68513-315-3 (Paperback); 978-1-68513-366-5 (Hardcover)
PUBLISHED BY BLACK ROSE WRITING
www.blackrosewriting.com

Printed in the United States of America
Suggested Retail Price (SRP) $19.95 (Paperback); $24.95 (Hardcover)

Accustomed to the Dark is printed in Minion Pro

*As a planet-friendly publisher, Black Rose Writing does its best to eliminate unnecessary waste to reduce paper usage and energy costs, while never compromising the reading experience. As a result, the final word count vs. page count may not meet common expectations.

ACCUSTOMED TO THE DARK

For Sheryl

ONE

2022

It was the break I needed. To land an interview with AJ Kenton was a journalist's dream. At the time I didn't know why he chose me to interview him, but there I was, twenty-four years old and driving to his home, moments away from meeting the famous recluse. And if I were lucky, I would uncover a story from our meeting, a story never told before. Well, I *was* lucky, but it wasn't the story I'd expected or wanted.

The author and artist used his hometown, Kenton, as his pen name, and as I turned off the highway and drove into the town center, the place looked exactly as I had imagined, as if suspended in time. Its four square blocks still had a bank, a diner, a hardware store, and a handful of other shops. There were ballfields, schools, a park with a bandshell, churches, and a synagogue, but mostly it was a town of houses built not long after the second world war. Today the town links to AJ Kenton, the creator of children's books, in the way Stockbridge links to Norman Rockwell. Because of that, the town gets its share of tourists, even though Mr. Kenton hasn't produced a book in thirty-three years.

My GPS guided me to the address, the same address jotted on a scrap of paper that, along with pens, writing pads, phone, and recording devices, sat on the passenger's seat. The steep driveway of dirt and stones leading up to the artist's house was a daunting sight, so instead of trying to motor my car up the incline, I shut off the Corolla's engine and parked on the street. The trek was tough because I hauled all my equipment while my two-inch heels kept sliding on the loose stones, but the interview, I told myself, would be worth it. After all, AJ Kenton was not only a national name, he was also a personal hero.

Like millions of children, his books were my first independent readers. More than that, his books inspired me to write. Not fiction, I admit, but journalism at least. I report the real world, but like many people I'm drawn to the world he created in his eleven books: a small town in the early 1960s; a time that most people today long for; a time when people faced simple conflicts and enjoyed happy endings. Those elements comprise the heart of his writing and the charm of his illustrations, which he also created. From what my older colleagues tell me, Kenton's books are a tribute to his boyhood as Mark Twain's *Tom Sawyer* is a hymn to his boyhood. And yet, Twain's story includes robbery and murder, both dark elements; whereas Kenton's books include no enduring darkness. His stories aren't as popular today— haven't been for years—but some kids still read them.

With spring just beginning, I had spent little time in the sun, so I wore a pink linen blouse to reflect color onto my face. My brown hair was cut short and my dark-rimmed eyeglasses, I hoped, produced a mature effect. I hiked up the drive to where a flagstone path on my left led to the front door of a Federal-style home. The door, siding, shutters, and roof were in terrible shape, and I wondered why a wealthy man lived in shabby conditions when a voice stopped me.

"Miss Smith?"

To my right a man rose from a wrought-iron patio chair with its twin on the opposite side of a round table. The sturdy furniture made a stark contrast to the man's appearance. He was tall but thin. He wore a denim shirt and ragged jeans. His sparse white hair almost matched his skin color, and his only facial hair, a trim mustache, looked like the ones men sported in old black-and-white movies.

"Mr. Kenton," I said and walked straight to him, extending my hand. He shook it, and I felt more bones than flesh. "Call me Jenny."

He asked if I had found his place all right and we volleyed small talk for a few minutes while I studied him closely. He would turn seventy-two in June, yet he looked and sounded older, his skin was creased and his voice craggy. But his eyes—of course it was his eyes— drew me in. They were gentle and lucid.

Looking into his warm eyes, I asked respectfully, "From all the journalists out there, why did you pick me for this interview?"

"I read your profile and liked your working-class background," he said. With a curious smile he added, "Most of all, I liked your name."

At the time it was an odd comment, but later I understood.

I settled into the surroundings quickly. Bordering the house, after a patch of lawn, was a stretch of forest turning green after a dreary winter. It was a perfect April day with a blue sky, puffy clouds, and a nice breeze, so with the pretty setting and this soft-spoken man, I felt at ease.

"We're far from summer," he said, "but I wanted lemonade this afternoon." His hand motioned to the table. "I brought out a pitcher of it and two glasses." Sheepishly, he admitted, "It took two trips." Then he asked if I'd pour.

I did and was glad for the cool drink after my long ride. "Hey, this is great."

"It's easy to make. Just lemons, water, and sugar. I don't know why people insist on those ready-made products."

"I guess it saves time."

"Yes," he said and looked away, dropping his voice, "we are consumed with and by time."

Beyond us was a rotting flower bed but with new shoots piercing the soil. Past the bed stood an oversized, weather-beaten shed. I had heard about that shed from the magazine's old-timers. After waiting as long as I could, I pointed to it. "Is that your studio?"

"Yes," he said without glancing at it. "The previous owner used it as a workshop. He filled it with many wonderful tools, but I converted the space into a studio where I could write and paint. I gave away the old tools—found them good homes— but one thing I kept was a handmade cradle. The man built the piece himself. You can see the care he put into it. Fine craftsmanship. A pity it was never used. I have no practical need for the cradle, but I just couldn't give it away."

I nodded toward the studio. "You must have added all those windows."

"Yes. I wanted to catch sunlight from the east, west, and south." He took a quick look at the shed and added: "That gate-door is original."

"I'd love to have a look inside."

"Perhaps later, Jenny. It's locked and the key is inside my house."

"I understand. But wasn't it in that shed where you drew your pictures and wrote your stories?"

"All but the first book."

My heart thumped. Here was the place where a set of beloved books had originated, and here was the man who had brought joy to so many people. Eager to begin the interview, I asked if it was all right to start recording and did so after he gave a silent nod. "That first book," I said, "you dedicated to your mother and father."

"That's right."

I checked my legal-sized notepad, knowing I'd prepared a bunch of questions, but actually asking them made me unsteady. Because I wanted everything to be perfect and didn't want to offend the man, I could feel my adrenalin turn to doubt. But this was my chance, so I pushed ahead. "From what I've read, your parents had a strained relationship, and one day your mother walked out and never returned."

"You found that on the internet, I suppose."

"Yes, I did, Mr. Kenton."

I was about to ask follow-up questions: Did you ever try to find your mother? Why did you leave home at such a young age? But impatiently he said, "You realize 'Kenton' is not my real name?"

"Yes."

"Right. AJ Kenton is the person who created illusions. He's nothing more than a sideshow magician who pulls a card from his sleeve. No," he stated as if summing up an argument, "AJ Kenton never told the truth. He told stories and drew pictures that people wanted."

"I don't understand."

"You will. Jenny, this really isn't an interview. This is not about your asking questions; it's about my telling one last story. And I need to tell it. You see, I shut the door on people, and that's my biggest regret. I should have been kinder. So, I want to tell a final story, but the telling will take a long time." He raised his eyebrows, as if expecting an answer.

"I have all afternoon."

"You'll need several afternoons."

That caught me off-guard, but I couldn't blow this chance. Besides, I had to prove myself to the established staff, which was primarily men. "I'll make time."

"Good, because *my* time is in short supply."

Suddenly, I knew. By the way he looked and spoke, I knew he didn't have long to live. So, I dropped my notepads and pens on the ground. After checking to see that both recorders were working, I set my hands on the hem of my skirt that touched my knees. "I'd like to hear your story," I told him. "No matter how long it takes." He nodded once and looked off to the budding trees.

"I was twenty-five years old when I returned to my parents' house after being away for nine years. The mortuary workers collected my father's body several days before I arrived, so I never saw what he looked like when the lung cancer took his life. He had asked for and received a closed coffin at the wake.

"I stood like a stranger inside my old house. I wanted nothing from it. No possessions of any kind. But on the kitchen table I found an envelope with my name on it. Then I uncovered another envelope. I never told anyone about them, but they changed everything."

"But that's pretty much what your bio says. After your father's death your career began."

He drank lemonade and cleared his throat. "I suppose that version works, Jenny, but I want to tell you more. You see, sometimes it takes awhile for the darkness to alter."

Over the next three afternoons we sat in the same wrought-iron chairs for several hours and I recorded every word. The weather held each day, but his strength failed by four o'clock. It may have embarrassed him, but I helped him inside every day. In the late afternoon on that first day, I found a motel along the highway five miles out of town.

During three afternoons with AJ Kenton, I discovered more about the famous man's life than I ever wanted to know. And because of that, I faced a dilemma: should a journalist's duty reveal the truth, or should a person's emotions conceal it?

TWO

My father's death was not the beginning. It was the end of a complex chapter. The beginning came with the start of 1963 in mid-January. Halfway through that winter month and into early spring, everything changed because, as a thirteen-year-old boy, I came across a set of circumstances I couldn't control. Added to that, my quiet personality played a role in the transition. By nature I'm an inward person. Coupled to that disposition was the part assigned to me within my family's dynamics. I felt overlooked and overshadowed by my parents' battles, so I conditioned myself to be an observer. I learned to listen. I learned not to state my thoughts.

I applied this approach not only to my family but also to the world beyond. As I interacted with others, by keeping quiet, people assumed I was nonjudgmental, so they thought me trustworthy. They thought I could bear witness to their deepest feelings and never reveal what

I'd been told. And I did nothing to discourage their beliefs.

And so, it started one afternoon. With a vile wind stinging my face, the one-mile walk home from school was miserable, but at least I remembered to take my hat, scarf, and gloves that day. Although the morning sky had been clear, by noon a cold front had descended into a frigid fog. By afternoon, a Northeast winter made its appearance. On my way home, I imagined my mother in the kitchen filling a mug with steaming cocoa and handing it to me. But I told myself not to count on that. For weeks she'd been acting strange and, like the season, closing herself off, as if securing a lid over a metal pot. Tension between my mother and father had been ratcheting. Because my father could be rigid, I knew he was the heart of my parents' problems.

I made it home, entered through the side door, and stood inside the kitchen where I felt the welcome difference from the outside. But when I removed my hat, scarf, coat, and gloves, I realized the house wasn't warm at all, and of course, no mug of hot chocolate waited. Our empty, dim kitchen felt as lonely and dark as an empty tomb.

"So, you're home." Without warning, my mother slipped into the room wearing a scruffy blouse with its faded floral design, a pair of old jeans, and a colorless sweater. As always, clothes covered her from neck to ankles. Silently, we stood, glanced at each other, and then looked away. I wanted her to say something, to ask me something—even about school—but her gaze was as barren and distant as space. I'd seen that expression before. Lost and searching for something, but that something always remained beyond her reach.

I pushed my hands into my pockets. "The walk home was really cold."

"Oh."

"Yeah. I thought maybe you could make hot chocolate?"

Briefly, she glanced around. "We don't have any." After a dull moment and feeling like an intruder, I started for the hall.

"Wait," she said, "I just remembered." I turned back with a spark of hope, but she moved to the counter and grabbed two envelopes. "The postman delivered the Billings' mail to our house. Take these next door."

I didn't want to go outside again and was about to say so, but her face hardened and her eyes didn't blink. I took the mail: a business letter from New York City and a pink envelope with fancy handwriting postmarked from Georgia. That was Mrs. Billings' home state. I put on my coat and gloves.

"Give them their mail and see if they have ours."

I walked to the door, turned back to say, Okay, but she had left the room.

Outside, although the sun shone weakly, the wind grew stronger and the temperature dropped. I moved fast. The Billings' home, a sprawling split-level, dwarfed our small ranch house. More than once I'd heard my father say, "Why do they have such a big house, especially with no kids?" Mr. Billings was president of our local bank. Our town, four miles away, was more of a village, so it needed only one bank. In his mid-forties, Brad Billings seemed to relish his unofficial title of Squire, which allowed him to be complacent and condescending. He wore three-piece suits, tailored shirts, and expensive ties. And he had an annoying habit of checking his gold pocket-watch during one-on-one conversations. But his wife was different. Susanna Billings was genial, charming, and artistic. At her request, her husband hired workmen to transform one bedroom into an art studio. Folks in the neighborhood agreed that Susanna Billings had talent for creating provocative work with oils, watercolors, and charcoals.

A minute after I rang the bell, Mrs. Billings opened their white-painted door, recognized me, and smiled. Her face, flecked with freckles, had a glow to it, and her straight, auburn hair fell at least a dozen inches below her shoulders.

"Well, well, who is at my doorstep? Why, I do believe it is my young and handsome neighbor." She had a way of making me blush, especially with a Southern accent, which we both knew was often exaggerated. "Come in, AJ, come in. That wind is sharper than a soldier's sword." I stepped inside and after she shut the door, I instantly felt the house's warmth.

I raised the Billings' letters to my chest. "I brought your mail."

With a laugh she said, "Has my young friend become the Postmaster General?"

I explained the situation.

"I see. Well, young sir, I have not retrieved our postal delivery today. Would you mind checking the mailbox for me?"

I didn't mind, not for her. Sure enough, inside their box was our mail. I recognized our heating bill and telephone bill, but on each envelope was something I hadn't seen before. Stamped in big red letters was the word: "Delinquent." Along with the bills was a colorful flyer, but it was so cold outside, I tucked everything under my arm and hurried back to the house. I showed her that, indeed, our mail had ended up in their box. Examining our bills, her eyes narrowed and her lips tightened, but after a moment she looked at me and smiled.

"Well, young neighbor, I was just about to make myself some hot chocolate when you came calling." Then her thick accent thinned. "Would you like some?"

I nodded eagerly.

"Hang your coat over there." She pointed to a cluster of wooden pegs.

I hung my coat and balanced my gloves on top of two pegs, and we set off for the kitchen.

"A day like today," she announced, "calls for hot chocolate. In fact, it is my belief that every day calls for some form of chocolate."

Their kitchen was twice the size of ours. With its white sink, white cabinets, and white appliances, the room could have been stark, but Mrs. Billings had broken the blankness by setting big glass jars on the counters and filling them with colorful spices. An oversized clock with a blue-stained, wooden frame hung on a wall, but what made the room especially warm were several framed watercolors positioned everywhere. Her unique artwork juxtaposed antithetical images: a weathered barn and a city diner; cornfields and tea packets; trees and row houses. The odd images somehow complemented each other. Her light and lively kitchen was such a contrast to ours.

As we stood there, she put a finger to her chin and looked puzzled. Then snapping her fingers as if to say, Oh, I remember she opened an upper cabinet door and then stood tiptoe to reach a salt-glazed canister. As she stretched and grasped the container, her slacks pulled tight against her tapered legs. Then she moved gracefully about, gathering everything needed and setting things in place. Next, she filled a copper kettle with water, and as she stood by the sink, a sliver of winter light sifted through the window. Her sheer white blouse revealed the shape of her naked breasts. It was safe to say that Susanna Billings dressed and acted differently from every woman in the neighborhood. After setting the kettle to boil, she leaned against the counter where lingering sunlight framed her unfettered hair.

"How was school today?"

"Fine."

"You're in eighth grade, right?"

I nodded. A moment later she poured hot water into two cream-colored mugs, each filled with spoonfuls of cocoa mix. We sat at a rectangular table, a farmhouse piece that could seat six. It was painted the same blue as the clock's frame and like the frame, the table had plenty of distress marks. As we sipped hot chocolate, for the first time since leaving school, I felt warm inside.

As my neighbor rested her chin in one palm, her bold blue eyes focused on me. "So, AJ, what school subject do you like least?"

It was a peculiar question but I had an answer. "Math." I set my mug down. "It's hard."

"Mmm. Same for me. Math and I are practically strangers. So then, what is your favorite subject?"

"Reading. I like stories about people."

"Real stories or made-up stories?"

"Both."

"Ah. Now, give me an example of a story you liked."

"Today we read about Michelangelo and how he painted the Sistine Chapel."

"My old friend, Michelangelo."

"Friend?"

She laughed and waved her hand. "Don't be so literal."

I smiled. "I was just joking."

"Uh hah! Now tell me, what did you like about the story?"

I clamped up because what I wanted to say wouldn't sound right. Oh, I could talk about baseball or fishing like any other boy, but not about something most boys didn't care about. Not even my parents—especially my father—would understand. But her sincere expression seemed to say, *Go on, tell me. Trust me.*

"I liked how he worked for so long and didn't quit. And he made something beautiful."

She raised an eyebrow and set her cup on the table. "AJ, have you drawn or painted pictures before?"

Embarrassed, I turned my head. "I've drawn some pictures."

"Do you like to draw?"

"Yes."

She murmured something under breath and waited until I looked at her again. "Well, my young and handsome neighbor, come with me."

We turned out of the kitchen, came to a set of split stairs, and climbed to the upper level. After walking along a carpeted hallway, we stopped at the farthest door. Opening it, she said, "My fortress."

The space dazzled me. I gazed at all the art materials: easels, brushes, small glass jars, charcoal sticks, paint, cloths, and canvases in various stages of completion. One showed an Old World setting where a milkmaid carried two pails attached to a yoke across her shoulders, but they weren't pails, more like balls that sagged to the earth and strained the girl's balance. An oil painting showed a wooden bridge that spanned two settings: a cityscape and a countryside. Another, a charcoal sketch, showed the backside of a naked woman—looking much like Mrs. Billings—sitting and adjusting her long hair. The smells and sights melded into a magical, alluring realm. I stood motionless. Then, her hand touched the small of my back and nudged me forward.

"Enter."

She guided me to a blank canvas propped on an easel. After grasping a tapered brush, she dipped its bristles in water, and then rolled the wet fibers against a tiny mound of paint. "Watch."

Her slender fingers held the wooden handle and without hesitation the brush dabbed and stroked the canvas. In about three minutes she painted a mug just like the ones we'd held in the kitchen. A band of steam swirled over it. The most amazing part was how the image suggested reality but wasn't quite real. Lines were loose yet firm; blurred yet sharp.

"Wow." The word fell out of me.

She took a step back. "Ta dah." Then she held the brush toward me. "Give it a whirl."

I must have gulped loud enough for her to hear it. "I'm not sure."

"Picture the object you want to create," she directed, "as if it were already there on the canvas."

Trying to imitate her movements, I took the brush and dipped its tip into the water jar, swished it, and then rolled the bristles against a tiny purple mound. I brushed a few strokes, and then I brushed more. She moved close to me, so close that I smelled a trace of scented soap.

"Let your hand flow." Her guiding words tingled my ear. "It's you, but it's also the brush." I kept at it until a flower—an iris—took shape. "That's it," she whispered. "Yes, your fingers and brush are one." Her lips hovered by my ear so that her breath beat against my flesh. I tensed. "Don't stop." She stepped back and I continued.

After a moment, my mind ascended into a higher dimension that I didn't know—although I'd come close to it before— actually existed. I was in myself and beyond myself. I was the actor and the audience, the art and the artist.

After shaping the iris as well as I could, I stopped and my body swayed. To steady me, Mrs. Billings held my shoulders. "AJ, that was wonderful." I tried to look at her but couldn't. "Hey," she said as if waking me from a hypnotist's trance, "let's return to the kitchen."

We sat in the same chairs and even though the hot chocolate had turned cold, I drank it. For a moment she looked at me while I stared at the table. At last she said, "I'm going to tell you something, AJ, and it's not to make you feel good nor is it insincere. You have talent and you must pursue it." She tapped the table gently. "You must see where your talent takes you. Do you hear me?"

"Yes, but…"

"But what?"

"I don't know." My face flushed.

"For goodness' sake, what would hold you back?"

I shrugged my shoulders.

Her thick Southern accent returned. "I should like my young and handsome neighbors to look at me when they speak—or shrug." I looked at her. Now her tone lowered. "So, tell me why you wouldn't pursue a God-given talent."

"It's not what guys do. Men are lawyers or bankers, firemen or policemen."

"I see." Susanna Billings nodded deliberately and then spread her ten fingers wide on the table. "I've been dealing with that nonsense forever. Conformity and conventions: what to wear, what to think, who to be! Well, I avoided those traps!" She stopped abruptly, calmed herself, and closed her fingers into loose fists. "But I've paid a price for 'a room of one's own.' Yes, a darkness for the light." She looked toward the window, blew out a long breath, and then looked back to me. "I hope someday people will have real choices instead of trying to fly with wax wings. I hope someday people will know it's all right to be different. And I'm not talking about trivial things like dyeing one's hair blue. Do you understand?"

"No."

She half smiled. "Right. Well then, let's get to the heart of it. Do you enjoy painting?"

"Yes."

"Of course you do. I can tell. As I said, you have a natural talent." She fingered auburn locks from her forehead and leaned toward me. Her eyes joined mine. "AJ, don't let others decide what you can or cannot do. Does *that* make sense?"

I nodded.

She looked at me as if taking stock of something. "Would you like to come here and paint? It would be our secret. At times I could mentor you, at times we could work together, and at other times I could leave you alone to explore and discover for yourself. Would you like that?"

"Yes," I said, "if it's all right with you."

"It's all right with me."

The simple moment passed. A moment of chance and circumstance. A muted, life-altering moment.

As I walked home I didn't feel so cold and decided to visit Mrs. Billings once a week. As a teacher, she was helpful and caring. As an artist, she had consigned me to a new world.

When I neared my house, the wind cracked and whipped and made me shiver, so I clutched the mail to my chest and slogged ahead. I stepped through the side door and entered the kitchen to find the room empty. After being in the Billings' house, my home looked and felt forlorn. A musty smell filled the place and our tiny wall clock ticked against an eerie silence. Dust glazed the counters, but it wasn't dust exactly because even dust is alive. The yellow linoleum floor and brown appliances and knotty pine cabinets looked tired, as if they had served their sentence and implored reprieve. It was four-thirty. My father would be home in an hour. My mother would start dinner. If I went to my room, I could be alone for awhile, and I didn't mind being alone.

I set the mail on the counter, this time taking a closer look at the flyer and was surprised to find it was sent to me. The US Seed Company offered a shrewd project. Their plan was to enlist kids to go door-to-door in their neighborhoods and sell packets of seeds. Each packet cost twenty-five cents. In return, the kids pocketed ten cents per sale; however, the money could only be redeemed by purchasing a product from the company's very own catalogue.

Excited, I plopped down on one of the painted chairs by the kitchen table and flipped through the catalogue's pages. The prize section showed items from sewing kits to baseball gloves. Of course, for the expensive items you needed to sell more packets. I turned the pages but stopped after spotting a paint set. It was a metal case in the shape of a ruler that snapped open or shut and protected ten tiny mounds of different colored paints. The kit included two brushes. My thoughts raced. I could visit Mrs. Billings and learn from her, and if I sold seeds and earned the Artist's Starter Kit, I could paint at home, too.

But I couldn't keep the kit in my room because my father would see it and that would lead to who-knows-what, so our basement was the answer. Our house had a half-basement with a water heater, a furnace, and storage space. We kept Christmas decorations in boxes down there, but this year everything stayed packed away because my mother said she didn't want the aggravation of setting things up only to take things down two weeks later. Because the basement measured five feet from floor to ceiling, no one went there without a reason, so I could secretly set up a small art space for myself. I double-checked the paint set's price and figured how many seed packets I'd need to sell. I smiled because a plan was falling into place. All I had to do was fill out a form and send it in, but I also had to choose which seeds to sell: vegetables or flowers.

"What's that?"

I nearly fell off my chair. My mother had a way of passing through the house like a wispy cloud. "A seed catalogue."

"Did you get our mail?"

"It's on the counter."

After picking up the two utility bills, she laughed—a short, sarcastic laugh—then placed the envelopes by the sink, face up.

Seeing my chance to escape, I took the catalogue straight to my room. Mine was the smallest room in the house, a narrow space with one narrow window. A twin bed and lowboy dresser filled the floor, leaving no room for a desk, which meant doing homework on the edge of my mattress. I tossed the seed catalogue on top of the dresser and turned to my math assignment. On page fifty-seven we were to solve the odd-numbered problems. As I sat on the bed, balancing a book, paper, and pencil on my lap, and because math stymied me, I lost interest, glanced at the catalogue, picked it up for a few minutes, and then started the process over again. When I wasn't looking at the catalogue, my thoughts drifted from the math problems to an image of selling packets to neighbors. I wondered where my quest would take me.

Surprised, I heard my father's car rumble up our gravel driveway, but the captain's clock on my dresser showed he was on time, and I realized my homework effort hadn't been productive, which meant I would spend more time after supper working those boring math problems. In order to hatch my plan, I'd bring the seed catalogue to the kitchen but wait a few minutes to let my father settle in, meaning he'd pour himself a beer and drink half of it before dinner. As for meeting my mother, my parents hadn't been interacting much lately—usually one syllable words and vague gestures— so I didn't need to give them time together.

When I reached the kitchen my father stood by the sink, looking out the window, as he did every day. He was of medium height but broad-shouldered with burly arms and stocky legs. He worked in a factory that made paints and varnishes where he manned assembly lines and forklifts and whatever else the plant's owners told him to do. His tasks usually called for strength. At his job and around the house he wore a work shirt, a T-shirt, and chinos; the smell of industrial lacquers embedded his clothes. Now, he held a glass of beer in one hand and the bills in another, yet he didn't look at either. He just stared through the window, mirroring my mother's earlier gaze, as if something out there was waiting for him.

"Hi, Dad."

"AJ."

My mother faced the stove, stirring a pot. Without turning, she said, "Set the table, AJ."

I put out knives, forks, and paper napkins. She set down bowls of spaghetti topped with marinara sauce— a bland, red liquid straight from a can. It was the third time that week we had spaghetti, which was bad enough, but worse was its complete lack of taste.

"It's food," my father told me as he took his seat and probably noticed my expression. "Eat your supper."

I sat opposite him at the square table where we ate all our meals. The table might have looked decent with a fresh coat of paint, but the old wooden piece, picked from a yard sale, never looked as if it were meant for family meals. As the norm had been lately, no one spoke. The only sound came from forks clacking against bowls. My mother had placed slices of untoasted Wonder Bread on a plate, but I chose not to eat the spongy stuff that night. One good thing about a terrible tasting meal: people don't take long to eat it. So, before my father left the table for the family room and television, I told him and my mother about selling seeds. He seemed interested and reached out a hand.

"Let's see that catalogue."

While he read through the guidelines, I glanced at my mother who had barely touched her food and now stared at the uneaten spaghetti.

"You get ten cents for every packet sold?"

"Yeah."

"Not bad." He looked toward my mother. "What do you think? AJ'd have to go door-to-door after school."

"He's old enough."

Out of nowhere, a fly darted past our faces, dived toward our bowls, and zipped frantic circles. My father waved the back of his strong hand at it. The fly was out of season but must have entered our house, hoping to find shelter until spring.

"Dad, which do you think I should sell, flowers or vegetables?"

"You can't sell both?"

"They make you choose one."

"Vegetables are more practical, but most people don't keep gardens anymore. Flowers aren't practical, but most people like them. It's your decision." He thumbed the catalogue's pages and came to the prizes. "What's this about?"

"After you sell the packets, you can get something from the catalogue."

"You don't keep the money?"

"No."

"Hah. How do you like that? Nice racket." His calloused hands held the booklet farther away so his near-sighted eyes could see the prizes better. "Well, I guess that's how business works." Then he pointed to a picture. "Hey, about this pocketknife? Would you like that? It has two blades, a corkscrew, scissors, and a bottle opener with a screwdriver tip." He waved at the annoying fly again. "A knife always comes in handy."

My mother muffled a laugh. Without raising her eyes, she said, "Why would a boy in today's world need a pocketknife?"

With a violent motion, my father raised his right hand, palm open, and swatted hard toward her face. She jerked back as his hand came close to her cheek and sliced the air. Breathing fast, she shoved her chair from the table, stood up, and glared.

"I was trying to hit that damned fly."

After pushing aside the wooden chair, she marched away.

My father watched her stomp off. "So stupid," he muttered. "I could just…" Then he looked at me, and there might have been guilt in his eyes. He sat there a moment before standing, hesitating, and then walking in the opposite direction.

What would I have done if he'd hit her? I don't know. As I cleared the table and put dirty things in the sink, I wondered what life would be like without him in our lives.

THREE

Two weeks later a box from the US Seed Company arrived with one hundred flower packets. I decided my father was right: most people didn't plant vegetables anymore, and although flowers serve no useful purpose, most people enjoy their beauty. On the day I began, school passed slowly because all I thought about was how to sell the seeds: where would I start and what would I say? I didn't know, but I decided that along with the cardboard box filled with packets, I would take a zippered pouch to collect coins from my sales.

During the next three months I rang dozens of doorbells. Most of the time I didn't make a sale; sometimes people invited me in for a cup of warm tea or cocoa. Nearly all the interactions were superficial—now forgotten—but the ones I'll tell you about have stayed with me. But Jenny, I've often wondered if, during those visits, people had something to say but chose to remain silent.

That afternoon, after rounding up what I needed, I felt excited to set off, but I wanted to see my mother first. I checked my parents' bedroom but she wasn't there. Or the kitchen. Or any room in the house. I called, "Mom," not too loudly but enough to startle a ghost. No answer. Finally, I went to the porch my father had closed in last summer. He installed cantilever windows with screens, found secondhand patio furniture, and bought a small black-and-white television so he could watch baseball games. Because the porch faced north, summer nights were fine, but winter days were brutal. Quietly, I opened the door to see my mother sitting hunched on a bamboo chair. She wore one sweater over another, leaned toward a window cranked halfway open, and blew cigarette smoke toward the icy metal screen. She told my father she'd quit smoking.

"Mom?" Her eyes grazed me warily before looking away. "I'm going now," I said. "To sell flower seeds."

"Okay."

I stood there, wanting her to say something—something about making sure I had everything I needed, about being careful, or about being proud of me.

"I'm a little worried because I've never done this before."

"What's the big deal? Either people buy or they don't buy."

"Yeah. I guess so." I turned for the door.

"You know it's Friday." Her face swiveled toward me. "Your father always brings pizza home on Fridays. Every Friday a large sausage pizza."

"I know."

"So, be home on time." She held the cigarette up and looked at it. "And you know what your father is like, so you know not to say anything about this, don't you?"

"Yes."

"All right, then." She waved her hand either to clear smoke or to send me away. "Go sell your flower seeds. Get a pocketknife. Maybe you'll skin a cat someday." She coughed without strength and hunched toward the window again.

I couldn't understand her. She was never a warm, effusive woman, but now she was cold and closed. Even with my father absent, she never lightened. And thinking about it, I realized he wasn't home much. By six forty-five each morning he'd leave the house, return at five-thirty, eat supper, and then, depending on the season, watch football or basketball or baseball on TV with a beer in his hand. Recently, he started working a half-day on Saturdays because of overtime. I asked my mother about overtime and she said it meant more money. She didn't seem pleased or displeased about that. Also, when the porch door shut behind me, I realized that nothing I could say to her would make a bit of difference.

My rubber boots bit into yesterday's snow, but today's sun felt good. However, the sun would set in a few hours so my selling time was scarce. I started with the Goldstein's house because Mr. Goldstein didn't work on Fridays and Mrs. Goldstein didn't work at all. At least not outside of the house, which in their case was one of the newer homes. My neighborhood could be divided into two sections: small ranch homes built before the war and larger homes built after the war. The later home-styles included split-levels, colonials, and raised ranches. The Goldsteins lived in a split-level. Their front yard was tidy and now their hedges, trees, flower beds, and hoary grass were glazed with snow—all waiting for spring. Soon after I rang the bell, Mr. Goldstein opened the door. He wore the same type of clothes as my father: gray trousers and a white T-shirt, but he also wore a navy cardigan sweater, unbuttoned. He was my father's height, about five feet nine inches, but he wasn't at all muscular.

"Hello, Mr. Goldstein."

"Hello, AJ. Are you out for a nature walk?"

"No, I…"

"What is that tucked under your arm? A box?"

"Well…"

"And there's writing on it?"

"Yes. It says…"

"I can see for myself if you would be kind enough to hold the package within my reading range." I lifted the box higher as he adjusted his horn-rimmed glasses. With an exaggerated tone of importance, he said, "The US Seed Company."

I wasn't sure why almost all of his sentences ended with an uplifted intonation, but I was sure the man meant no harm. His eyes glistened in a playful way while his words and gestures conveyed a lightness to them, as if he were sharing a secret laugh with you. His reddish hair was thinning to baldness.

"So," his thumbs curled into the belt loops of his trousers, "what is the purpose of your visit?"

After a deep breath, I let the words, which had been fluttering inside my brain, fly: "I'm selling packets of flower seeds. Would you like to buy some?"

"Ah hah. So, you're a bona fide peddler? And is that *it*?"

"What?"

"It, *it*! Is that your best sales pitch spiel? Shouldn't you say something like: 'This is a deal of a lifetime' or 'These flower seeds are seeds you cannot live without?'" He chuckled in a way that made me join in.

"I guess you could live without them," I said, "but flowers look nice in the summer."

"You have a point, young peddler. Come in."

Although their house was fairly new, the inside felt old. In the living room a heavy woolen fabric upholstered the sofa and chairs, and stitched doilies layered armrests and headrests. A braided, oval rug covered most of the wood floor. In the dining room, an oak curio-cabinet, table, and chairs were massive and dark.

"I was working a crossword puzzle," he said and motioned to the table. "Sit. Sit and show me your line of goods."

Anxiously, I opened the shipping box and set a half-dozen packets on the table. "Some flowers do great in the sun and some do good in the shade."

"Do well."

I looked up, confused.

"Not 'do good'; do *well*. And it just so happens it's a four-letter word that fits perfectly for number six across, even though the clue is for a wishing well." He quickly filled the crossword squares. "Now, show me flowers that do well in the sun." He smiled again and I grouped together four packets.

"These do *well* in the sun."

He bowed over the packs, revealing a bald spot on his head. "Yes," he said, "these three flowers I like. Beautiful. But I must consult my supervisor." He looked up, winked, turned his head, and called, "Sarah! Leave the cooking and come here. To an important business transaction we must attend."

His wife, a plump, sturdy woman wearing a tan blouse and long brown skirt, both almost hidden by a full-length apron, appeared. "Ah," she said, recognizing me, "hello, AJ." Then she looked at her husband and spoke with the same uplifting intonation. "And what is so urgent?"

"We must decide which flower packets to purchase. Very important."

"I see." Mrs. Goldstein smiled. "A Yankee peddler."

"Sarah, we're not in New England. The only Yankees near us are a baseball team. So, which flowers do you like?"

She moved closer. "How much are they? The packs."

"I didn't ask."

"You didn't ask? So *ask*!"

"Twenty-five cents apiece," I said.

"Oy." She put a hand to her chest. "Why so much?"

I explained the seed company's system and how, with my earnings, I'd probably get a pocketknife.

"I think every boy should have a pocketknife," Mrs. Goldstein said. Then she placed her hands on her hips and regarded me closely. "AJ, I've known you many years and I mean no disrespect, but a seller of goods you don't look like. Not with those soulful eyes. No, you don't look like a talker. More like a listener. Someone with empathy, at least." She turned to her husband. "Asa, you choose the flowers. The outside of the house is your side of the house. In the meantime, AJ, can I get you a glass of water or milk?"

"No, ma'am. Thanks anyway."

"In that case I will make use of this chair and read my *Saturday Evening Post*. I've made a nice salad that's sitting in the fridge, and in thirty minutes I'll fix the macaroni and cheese."

"Are you using three different cheeses?" Mr. Goldstein asked.

With a weary sigh, Mrs. Goldstein sat on the cushioned chair. "Twenty-one years we've been married, Dear God, and for twenty-one years I've used three different cheeses in my macaroni and cheese. Now my husband asks if I'm using three cheeses? I suddenly don't look like your wife?"

"For positive, you look like my wife. I'm only asking because I love your macaroni and cheese. In all the world, it's the best." He turned to me. "Do you like macaroni and cheese?"

"Sure."

"I'll bet you never tasted any as good as Sarah's. She uses three different cheeses, and in all these years she's never told me which three cheeses."

"Who says you need to know?" his wife asked. "You don't cook; you eat."

"This is true."

"Besides, it's not the cheeses that make the dish special so much as my secret ingredient."

"I almost forgot." He waved both hands in the air as if surrendering. "The secret ingredient. I couldn't possibly persuade you to divulge your secret ingredient?"

"Do I look like a pushover?"

"A pushover you're not."

"Then don't ask."

Mrs. Goldstein opened her magazine that featured a Norman Rockwell illustration on the cover. My agent tells me that people like my books because they're set in the past when the days were supposedly happier and simpler, but truthfully, those days were no different. Each was twenty-four hours long with an ever-altering division between light and dark.

"So," Mr. Goldstein said to his wife with a gentle laugh, "we'll wait patiently for your special dish." He looked at me again, but abruptly his expression changed. It reminded me of March weather that turns in an instant from sunshine to clouds. He looked as if someone had hurt his feelings. "Are you surprised that my wife and I eat macaroni and cheese?"

"No."

"Our son and daughter love it, too."

"Sure," I said and suddenly felt uneasy.

"Asa, he's only a boy. Stop. I know what you're doing."

"Mmm," he muttered and then continued in a softer tone. "AJ, because we're Jewish, people think we don't eat normal foods, that we eat toads or something crazy like that. They think we're pagans, that we dress in strange clothes, and that all Jewish men have long, dark beards."

Some of my friends *had* said vicious things about Jews. They even claimed that Jewish girls were physically different from other girls, and I should stay away from them.

"Asa, not everyone thinks those things, and no one thinks you have a long, dark beard. Not with that red hair of yours."

"Some people, when they first meet me, I tell them I'm Irish." He laughed and his laughter seemed to defeat his darkness. "You'll have to excuse me, AJ. With religion, sometimes I get carried away. I become the very people who frighten me: the ones who label, the ones who fear. I must tell myself to take my foot off the reigns."

His wife giggled. "Asa, you pull *in* the reigns. You take your foot *off* the gas pedal."

"Horses, cars—what's the difference?"

"Have you ever been on a horse?"

"No."

"*That's* the difference." She folded her magazine, set it on her lap, and after a pause, said, "Religion should give people a reason to love, not to hate."

"Love is stronger than hate," said her husband, "but love is hard; hate is easy."

"And people get so worked up over silly things." She raised her chin thoughtfully. "You know, when I was a young girl, my father told me about a story he'd read in a book. An old book. Some people in a faraway country were divided into two groups. And the two groups were fighting. And over what did they fight?" She raised her right hand. "God's truth. They fought over which end of an egg to crack open: the big end or the little end! My father said the argument was really about religion."

"*Gulliver's Travels.*"

"Who?"

"Gulliver. He traveled." Mr. Goldstein nodded. "That was the book, and during Gulliver's trips he came to a land of little people. Even though they were tiny people, they tied Mister Gulliver down. Anyway, with his voyages, he saw many strange things. Even horses that could talk."

"Did I say anything about horses?"

"You were talking about Gulliver."

"I was talking about eggs."

"Same thing. The point is, people look for the different when they should look for the similar."

"That's right. After all, an egg is an egg."

They looked at each other and burst out laughing in a way that anyone could tell happened often.

"AJ," he said, "should I tell you a secret? I'm not a strict Jew. Not like my two brothers. You know the three of us own the clothing store in town, Dad and Lad."

"Sure." My father had taken me there many times. "I like your store."

"Thank you, young peddler. Well, on Saturdays my brothers will not work, but I will. That's why I have Sundays and Fridays off. Saturdays and Sundays they have off, which is good because they live away in the city, and they have two days in a row without disruption. Sarah and left the city for a town because a better house we could afford. It's good, too, because here a traditional life we don't have to live, but it's bad because here not many Jews are, so we stick out like sore thumbs. Yes, some people look too hard for the different."

"Maybe someday," his wife said while scanning her magazine, "people won't care about which end of an egg to crack."

Then their two children rumbled down the stairs. I knew them—not well—but in this neighborhood all the kids knew of each other. Sam was a high school senior and Deborah a sophomore. She favored her father: lean limbs and reddish-brown hair. Her face was round and pretty with a small beauty mark on her left cheek. Her slender body showed a shapely figure. Sam, however, favored his mother, having dark hair and a solid frame. Everyone knew he was a star athlete and a standout student. Of course, my being in eighth grade set me apart from them.

After we exchanged hellos, Mr. Goldstein explained why I was there, and Deborah came to the table. "Let me choose a packet, Father."

"Your homework. It's finished?"

"All of it."

"Yes, of course." He wagged a finger. "Education is the key that…"

"Unlocks every door." Deborah finished his words before he could.

"You are following your brother's example? Valedictorian?"

"I'm trying, but Sam is a tough act to follow."

Her brother smiled. "Oh, you can do it, Deb. You're smarter than I am."

"I don't know about that." Her pretty face blushed. "So, what about these flowers?"

"Yes," her father said, "flowers, too, are important. Here, choose."

"These are nice." She held up a packet. "Zinnias. Hey, we can build a new flower bed by the front window and plant a bunch of these."

"Such an imagination from my beautiful daughter. And this new flower bed? Who will build it?"

"I will."

"*You* will? Without knowledge of nail and hammer?"

"Hammer, shmammer." She shrugged her shoulders. "I'll figure it out."

"So, a little help maybe I could give?" He gazed proudly at his daughter.

"Speaking of help," Mrs. Goldstein said and set the *Saturday Evening Post* on her lap, "Deborah, come help me in the kitchen. It's time to blend the three cheeses. And of course, we must add my secret ingredient."

"All right, Mother."

Even though she was two years older, as Deborah walked by, because she was pretty and because she couldn't be anything but physically normal, I tried to catch her eye. I did. Instead of ignoring me, dimples touched her cheeks as a smile lit her face.

"Yes, zinnias are a definite." Mr. Goldstein put a pack to one side of the table. "Sam, would you like to choose?"

"No, thanks, Dad. I have more studying to do. That Latin vocab is a killer."

Mr. Goldstein watched his son head upstairs. Then he turned to me and took a deep breath. "My father—God rest his soul—an educated man he was not, but he was perhaps the smartest man I will ever know. In life, he was a tailor, and as a boy, I wished to be a tailor like him. So, I learned from him, and I got pretty good. Not as good as him, but you could say I had the knack." He glanced at the crossword puzzle. "Today, for particular customers, I still mend clothing, and it's a good feeling to know that you can take something that is torn and make it whole again. But," he grabbed his pencil, "ah, twenty-two down: the 16th American President. Finally, an easy one." He jotted in an answer and dropped the pencil. "But some things are torn so badly that I can't fix them. And that hurts. You see, my father his whole life worked hard so his boys—and he only had sons—would have the step-up he never had. He made sure we had an education, at least through high school." He leaned toward me. "To tell you the truth, it was my father who said that education is the key that unlocks every door. But, of course, an education is not just knowing a world of truths; it's more about knowing truths of the world. The world right in front of you." Lightly, he tapped his pencil on the puzzle. "Too many people lock too many doors for other people. The ones with the keys want the others to stay out, so the locks remain, old and rusted. But I want for my children to unlock those doors. Who knows?" he shrugged. "A doctor? A lawyer? One of each?" His eyes watered a little, and then he clapped his hands as if to force his dark mood to shift. "Yes, yes. And now, we are in the middle of an important business transaction: flowers. These four packs I will purchase."

"Thanks, Mr. Goldstein." I was thrilled, having made my first sale.

"No need to thank me. These flowers I don't buy for myself, young peddler. They are for my children and my children's children. Everything I do is for them. For the family I know, and for the family I will never know."

He handed me four quarters and I dropped them into my zippered pouch. I smiled but wondered why Mr. Goldstein looked sad when he talked about his children's future. Then he ran fingers through his thinning hair. "Would you like to join us for supper? My

Sarah's macaroni and cheese is the world's best." Again, he leaned in confidentially. "That secret ingredient? Teeny-tiny bits of lobster," he whispered. "So, what do you say? Supper?"

"Thanks, that's really nice, but I'm going to try one more house before going home."

"I see. An enterprising young man you are? Very well."

After saying my goodbyes, I stepped outside. The sun was setting and winter shadows gathered, so I headed to Mrs. Warren's house, which was nearby and exactly the same type of house as the Goldstein's because—as my father had told me—the same builder constructed both. But coming up to her house, instead of seeing a well-kept property like the Goldstein's, I saw a patch of weeds bordered by unruly bushes and untamed vines that traversed the ground, clung to trees, and tangled bare limbs, as if some giant creature had knitted a snare.

Everyone called her *Mrs.* Warren even though no one had seen her husband for years. Almost triumphantly, my mother told me that one night Mr. Warren went out for a pack of cigarettes and never returned. She had a special laugh for that story. For the past five years Mrs. Warren worked as a cashier at the A&P. Whenever I went there with my father, we usually wound up in her lane, and he made me help her bag our groceries. She'd thank me in a quiet way, and from what I could tell, this reticent woman never seemed happy yet she never seemed unhappy. She seemed empty.

Throughout the grocery transaction, she spoke the fewest words possible.

As I approached her house, the pounding beat of rock music, at first faint, grew louder. Standing by the front door, I recognized the song "Great Balls of Fire" by Jerry Lee Lewis. If I tried the doorbell, she wouldn't have heard me, so I waited until the music stopped. Then I rang the bell and followed with two firm knocks. After a brief wait, the door opened. Mrs. Warren wore a white headband, a sleeveless gray T-shirt, red gym shorts that touched the middle of her thighs, and a pair of tennis shoes. Her clothes were sweat-soaked, her face was florid, and she was breathing hard.

"AJ?"

"Yes, ma'am."

"What are you up to?"

I told her. Her dark eyes examined me and the box I held. After hesitating, she said, "Come in."

I followed closely because the house had no lights on. Her dark hair, pulled into a ponytail, bobbed against the back of her wet shirt. We walked to the living room where no lamps shone, but winter light gleamed through the expansive picture window and suffused the room with a crimson glow. We sat on mismatched, uncomfortable wooden chairs.

"I was exercising," she explained. "I've been doing that for a few years now. It's important to keep in shape, you know?"

I nodded, but back then most women didn't exercise like that, if at all, so it was queer to see a woman dressed that way and sweating that way. But I had to admit, she looked alive, unlike the way she looked at the A&P. But I wouldn't say Mrs. Warren was beautiful or even pretty; although there was something about her furtive eyes and sad expression that could lure a person.

"I thought of joining a gym and taking exercise classes," she said, pulled off her sweatband, and tossed it on the table, which was a piece of square, beveled glass resting on chrome legs, "but that costs money so I made up my own class." She spoke quickly and not necessarily to me because her eyes wouldn't settle. Nervously, she touched her hair or plucked the damp T-shirt from her skin. We sat inches apart, but it felt like she was talking to herself, as if revealing one side of a conversation that had been careening inside of her for a long time.

"Exercise. Did you know for years I was overweight? Yes, indeed. A plump turkey ready for slaughter." She smiled mechanically. "But I changed. Changed everything: eating, drinking, smoking. And I read about exercise—how important it is—and then an idea hit me: play hard-ass rock and roll. Whoops." She looked at me. "Excuse my language, AJ."

"That's okay."

"Sure. You've probably heard worse. Maybe in the school hallways?"

"Yes, ma'am."

"Well, that's what I do five nights a week. Play loud rock music and dance to it. No set steps, mind you, but I shake, rattle, and roll for one whole hour. You caught me just when I finished." She had carried a hand towel into the room and now wiped her face and patted her upper chest as perspiration popped from her pores. Because she had been exercising, she must have set the thermostat awfully low, so I felt the room's chill.

Sitting to her right, I set my box on the table and noticed the sun's dipping rays illuminating her face. Then she looked at me in the way a cat might look at a ball of twine.

"So, you're selling flower seeds. Why?"

I told her about the rewards program and how I would probably choose a pocketknife.

"Careful you don't cut yourself," she smirked, "especially if you keep that knife in your pocket." Then, without warning, she roughly pushed herself from the table. "I need water. You want a glass?"

"All right, thanks."

As she made her way to the kitchen, I laid a few seed packets on the cold glass tabletop and thought how differently Mrs. Warren was behaving from the person who passively rang the cash register and barely said two words as she bagged groceries. Here, she was more animated, yet something was out of joint.

I heard tap water run and then a clinking sound. Returning, she handed me a glass of water with two ice cubes floating in it. She must have been thirsty because she drank half her glass in one gulp.

"Water is the only fluid we need. Did you know that?"

"No."

"Yes, indeed. Our bodies are mostly water."

I wanted her to look at the seed packets, but her eyes jumped from the picture window to the brick fireplace to the mantel clock to the empty sofa. After undoing her ponytail, she sat erect, and raked fingers through her dark, straight hair. I wondered why she talked about exercise and water and couldn't focus, and then I wondered if Mrs. Warren had anyone to talk *to*. She'd been living alone for years.

"Yes, indeed," she said under her breath. "There was a time when I drank everything *but* water." Then she giggled like a girl. Abruptly she stopped, as if remembering I sat beside her. "Watch out for alcohol, AJ," she said in a level tone. "It's the devil's brew, and liquor grants no mercy. Got that?"

"Yes, ma'am." I stretched my fingers toward the flower packets, and the movement, as I had hoped, caught her attention.

"Oh, such pretty pictures. Those flowers look perfect." She bent forward to see better because the sun was setting. But then her concentration ceased as she sank back in her chair and went limp. Suddenly, some strange transformation happened. It was as if a wretched specter invaded her, as in a low-budget movie where someone speaks in a peculiar voice: cold and distant. "You know, nothing turns out that way: perfect. It's all brainwashing. All bullshit. Everything from pictures on cake mixes to happy endings in books. It's all a lie. But we keep buying. Load after load of bullshit. Well, I stopped buying. Oh, it took awhile, but I stopped."

She gazed straight ahead at something, but I couldn't tell what it was. I drank more water but my throat stayed dry. Everything—her voice, her mood, the chill, the darkness—felt eerie. I stood and started picking up the packets. "You don't need to buy anything, Mrs. Warren. And it's getting late, so I'd better go." Then her hand touched mine.

"Wait," she said. "I didn't mean to…. Sit down, AJ. Please."

She looked like a lost child, so I sat down.

"Mrs. Warren," she echoed. "Yes, indeed, everyone calls me Mrs. Warren, but that person is dead. And so is Miss Stillwell. She disappeared ages ago. So, what do I call myself now?" She sipped her water, looked away, then looked at the packets. "Those pictures *are* beautiful, and with enough rain and sun, the flowers should grow just fine." She bowed her head. "Sorry, AJ. I'm tired. Long day, you know?"

"Yes, ma'am."

Now, all agitation seemed drained from her body. When she spoke, her voice was soft and her face serene, but she stared in a direction with no name.

"It hasn't been easy for me. Of course, I've made foolish choices, but you must understand how little I knew about…how things really are. No, I didn't understand the real world. I was more naive than young. Too naive when I married. I believed the fairytales—all those pretty little books I read as a girl. Yes, indeed. I bought the full line."

Without looking at it, she picked up a packet of daffodil seeds. I could barely see her fingers.

"My parents were old and lived on what was left of a family farm, but that way of life was dying fast. Each year they sold off more land, but each year they found themselves more in debt. If I married, I could leave home and ease their burden. That's all they cared about, so you can see why I married Rick. It had little to do with love."

Absently, she fingered the seed packet, dropped it, and picked it up again.

"Did I love Rick? Sure. Being young and excited and hopeful, I read articles in women's magazines and followed advice columns, trying to please him. And did I make plans? Oh yes, indeed. So many. The house we'd have someday, the children, and the wonderful lives we'd live. I created pretty pictures. Just as pretty as these packets."

She dropped the seeds and let the pack lie on the table. I wanted her to stop talking because it felt like I had stepped into a forbidden place, but I was too unnerved to say anything.

"The first year of marriage—year and a half—was mostly good. Physical. Very physical. We wanted children, but none came. Then things unraveled. The next three years were awful. For awhile we argued about everything. Some knockdown drag-outs. Did he beat me? Yes. To hide the marks, I became creative with clothes. But that phase passed, and in the next phase we hardly spoke. I knew that type of thing happened to other people, but I couldn't believe it was happening to me. But it was."

With every word and every minute, the space grew darker until I could barely see her. Her face became indistinct—the face that I later sketched to illustrate certain characters—and her voice: insipid yet seductive—a voice that centuries ago caused sailors to wreck ships and drown in mythological seas.

"Then one day, a beautiful spring day, Rick came home from work, packed two suitcases, and left. He had met someone. She was pretty and three months pregnant. Rick said he and I were lucky to make a clean break. It was better that way. Well, it was better for him, but what about me? No college. No family. No job. I was lost. Yes, I used to sit at this table and wait for him to return. I'd look to the window, the fireplace, the sofa, the clock. I'd listen for his car."

For an instant I thought I heard a car turn into her driveway.

"I had to fill long days and longer nights. Yes, indeed. So I drank. Vodka, mostly."

The room had stitched itself into a chilled darkness. I couldn't see her, but I felt her. Her disembodied voice embraced and enclosed me. It was if her soul had entered my body and my body had entered her soul. Perhaps I felt her heartbeat when a fearful memory came to me.

It happened last summer, and because of storm clouds and a new moon, the evening began in darkness and grew darker. Along with two friends, Kevin and Lee,

I met up with another friend, Frank, at his house. We bought sub sandwiches and Cokes and sat inside his family's screened-in back porch. We ate, laughed, and talked for hours. Then it was time to leave.

Frank lived near the center of town so we had a four-mile walk back, but that was the easy part. The trial came in crossing Route 22. The four-lane highway ran east-west and dissected Kenton about halfway to our homes. We could cross the road but that was tricky because you had to hop over a tall cement divider and, because the highway snaked and dipped, you couldn't see far in either direction. And traffic never stopped. It was rare for two sets of double lanes to be clear of traffic at the same time. It was a dangerous crossing.

Fortunately, at that point beneath the highway was an enormous, round drainage ditch, its circumference measuring five feet. The top and sides were galvanized steel while the bottom was dirt, stones, and water, water that ran fast with recent rain or lay stagnant during dry spells. It hadn't rained in a week, so that left a shallow spill on the ground. Between the two crossing options, we chose the tunnel.

When we reached the round opening, the atmosphere, as it often does before a summer cloudburst, turned still. We peered ahead, but the passageway was ink-black. With the starless, steamy night, the air within that tunnel felt thicker than fog. Scenes from old horror movies flashed in my mind. For a moment the three of us wavered at the opening, and perhaps we thought there was a better way to reach the other side. Finally, Lee walked ahead. Kevin followed and I was last. I moved cautiously, hoping my eyes would adjust to the lack of light. Then, about a third of the way through, something scurried and splashed by Lee's feet. "A rat!" he yelled.

Kevin yelled.

I yelled.

All at once, we ran.

Halfway through the tunnel I tripped, fell, and landed on my side. I was stunned but felt something scamper across the back of my neck. I jumped to my feet, but everything whirled in a circle. Lee and Kevin were gone. Their adrenaline must have jetted them far beyond the tunnel. I tried to step forward but staggered and bumped into the steel barrier. My hands reached out but there was nothing to touch, so fear and panic zipped through me. As I inched along, gradually the vertigo stopped and my sight adjusted. I made it to the other side just as Lee and Kevin returned, calling my name. I felt excited to be alive, and after I explained what had happened, we stayed close and hurried home before rain clouds burst.

"After three months of feeling dead—I remember it clearly—I woke up, looked out the window, and saw that the weather was miserable." Mrs. Warren spoke in an otherworldly voice. "A gray, misty, damp day, the kind of day that made me gloomy. But instead of feeling depressed, I felt as if a terrible weight had been lifted. I felt like a child on Christmas morning when a dizzy happiness dances through you.

"In the shower, I washed myself more than clean. I dressed for a new day. And for breakfast, I drove miles to the Sunrise Diner—a place I'd never been—and I ate more food and drank more coffee than any morning before or since. And sitting alone in a booth, with storm clouds in the sky, it came to me. My life wasn't ruined; it was saved. I realized for the first time I could do whatever I wanted and be whoever I wanted. It was powerful.

"So, I stopped drinking and started taking care of myself. Within a week I found a job at the A&P. I made a new life. All right, a small life, but it was *my* life. Yes, indeed. And I had time to think in ways I had never thought before. And after thinking about so many things, I understood the only person you can count on is yourself, and I faced the fact that only a handful of lives matter. Oh, we make a show of things with our cries and whispers, but most of us die without notice or sorrow."

I felt paralyzed in that icy room, listening to a lifeless voice and staring at a dim silhouette.

"I realized the things I once wanted were meaningless because I didn't need them anymore. The roles I'd wanted no longer mattered. I was completely free. I didn't need to be a wife, a spouse, or a mother. I wasn't tied to someone's dreams. Not even to Mrs. Warren's because that name was no longer a name. It was just a sound."

The room—the entire house—was lightless. Shadows had melded, and the table's glass top felt colder than a broken promise.

"Some people might say I've isolated myself, but I call it self-reliance. You see, I don't need a thing. Not friendship or love or even touch. Indeed. I have shelter and food. Food from the almighty A&P."

Then, when I wasn't sure if I was still breathing, she stopped speaking. Her seance-like trance ended as she shivered and looked around.

"What's happened? It's so dark." After bolting from her chair, she switched on the overhead light. I blinked from the brightness. "AJ, why didn't you say something?"

"I…I didn't know what to say."

"It's so damned cold," she whispered and crossed her arms beneath her breasts. Her cheeks were wet with tears. "Oh, AJ. I'm sorry."

"It's all right. I was just leaving," I said, embarrassed and already standing. "I'll pack up the seeds."

"Seeds? Oh, right, the flower seeds." She glanced at the packets. "Sorry, but I have no use for them. Maybe someday." Then waved a hand dismissively. "No. No, never."

"That's all right." I scrambled to put everything back.

"Wait." After dabbing her cheeks with the hand towel, her eyes brightened. "How much are they—the packets?"

"Twenty-five cents."

"Why don't I give you a quarter, and you can buy a pack for someone special? Your mother?"

My mother had never said whether she would buy any flowers. "Thanks, but you don't have to."

"I insist." She pointed over her shoulder. "There's spare change in my bedroom, and I need to raise the thermostat. Wait here, AJ. I'll only be a minute."

I waited longer than a minute, and when Mrs. Warren returned she wore tan slacks and a navy sweatshirt. "Here you go." She handed me a quarter. "Choose a pretty flower, and give it to someone special. Maybe flowers will give her hope."

Outside, evening webbed the neighborhood; however, yesterday's snow reflected moonlight, which made my way home easier. But the way didn't make my destination brighter. Walking along, I thought about Mrs. Warren's bizarre revelations and her wish for the packet of seeds, but the person who needed them most would never take them.

FOUR

"Why don't you buy some new clothes?"

My bedroom door was open, which made it easy to hear my parents arguing even though they were in the kitchen. They never shouted, and it was years later when I learned that shouting at someone requires a deeper level of regard. My father's tone was always practical, as if pleading a case for common sense. "Doesn't everyone want or need new clothes now and then?"

My mother's tone was indifferent. More so than ever, she seemed detached from everything. "I don't care about clothes."

"I'm not saying you should care about clothes like some people do. I'm saying that sometimes new clothes make a person feel better. Happier."

"Oh?"

I pictured my mother's sardonic expression.

"And what about the money for these new clothes?" she asked. "We're not the Rockefellers."

"I make enough for you to afford things."

"Right. Tell you what, why don't we wait until Christmas like we always do?"

"You wanted nothing for Christmas."

"And that's just what I got."

It was silent for a long moment. I pictured my father's hands forming fists. When he spoke again, his voice was tight, as if talking through his teeth. "You wear the same clothes every day."

"So?"

"They're worn out."

"So?"

"So, if you had new clothes maybe you'd get out of the house and *do* something."

"Oh, that's it? You want me to get a job."

"Who said anything about a job?" My father could have left it there, but he probably cocked his head and crossed his arms under his chest, the way he did when he directed something. "But if you *want* to get a job, that wouldn't be so bad."

"Ha! New clothes. What a load of shit! It's all about money, isn't it?"

"No."

Silence.

"And just where would I get a job in this two-bit town? The bank? The hardware store? The diner? Oh, I know—the A&P. I could stand on my feet all day and be like that pathetic Patty Warren, ringing the register and sacking eggs."

"This isn't about a job. I just thought you might want new clothes." He must have taken a few deep breaths.

"You're so miserable. I wish you'd do something about it."

"Don't worry. I'm just in a winter mood." Her voice now came from a farther distance—she must have left the kitchen—and she spoke without emotion. "Everything will change come spring. Everything."

***

"Well, well," Mrs. Billings said with a wide smile as I stepped inside her house, "my young artist has become a traveling salesman."

"Yes, ma'am." Even though I'd been seeing her once a week for art lessons, she always made me blush, not only because she was pretty, but because of her light and gentle spirit.

"I do hope you're not the Willy Loman kind. No, young sir, we'll have none of that nonsense here."

"No, ma'am," I said but didn't know what she meant.

She wore a chambray shirt that embellished her blue eyes and enhanced her auburn hair. The blouse's top two buttons were unfastened and its shirttails stayed untucked outside a pair of slim denim slacks. A curious aroma of oil paint and soft perfume floated from her.

"I can see this is not a social call but one of business. Fortunately, you are in luck because the man of the house is present. Mr. Billings works from nine til noon on Saturdays at the bank, so it's shrewd of you to call at this hour."

"You told me to stop by at this time."

"Did I? I don't recall saying any such thing." She winked. "Right this way, young sir."

Instead of going upstairs toward her studio, we dropped a level and walked to the opposite end of the house. The narrow hallway led to one room with its door ajar. Mrs. Billings softly knocked on the raised-panel wood, opened the door a few inches, and poked her head inside. She whispered something to her husband. Then she opened the door fully. "Be kind to him, darling," she said in a breezy way. "He's trying to be a man of business, like you." Turning, she winked at me again, and glided away.

"Come in, AJ." Mr. Billings spoke in a friendly but formal manner.

Since the curtains were pulled shut against each window, the room was dark, so it took my eyes a moment to adjust, and the study had a stale odor to it, a scent I couldn't recognize, but it struck me as unhealthy. He rose behind an imposing desk where he'd been working. As he stood there, I noted he was shorter than my father, and instinctively I compared the two men. They had little in common. While my father had a strong physique, Mr. Billings had a dumpy build, including a pot belly. Although he was only eight years my father's senior, he looked much older. He was bald to the top of his ears; then his gray hair was barber-trimmed. His bifocals appeared small against his round, full face, and his clothes looked more costly than anything my father ever wore: a white dress shirt and gray slacks that matched a suit jacket, which, along with a paisley necktie, hung on the top curve of a tufted, swivel chair directly behind his desk. The desk, made from cherry wood, had a flat surface about six feet long and two feet wide. In an orderly way, pencils, pens, a cigar box, envelopes, stationery, newspapers, a bottle of scotch, a glass tumbler, stamps, paperclips, and a calendar lay across the polished wood, all within his reach.

"Pull up that chair." He pointed to a wingback chair sitting kitty-corner between an oblong window and a dozen shelves filled with handsomely bound books. I glanced at the titles but didn't know them because they pertained to banking and finance. I did, however, recognize a complete set of the *Encyclopedia Britannica*. My school's library owned a set, but his set looked richer because of its leather binding.

"Can you manage that chair? It's not a lightweight."

"Sure," I said and set my box on the seat. After gripping the arms, I pulled, hoisted, and dragged the chair up to his desk. "You sure have a lot of books."

"Yes. I believe you will find exactly 387 books on those shelves."

"Wow! Have you read them all?"

"Hardly. But I didn't buy them for that purpose." He cleared his throat. "So, my wife tells me you've become a salesman." As I explained my plan, he nodded a few times and when I finished he said, "It doesn't matter what sort of *prize* you get: a pocketknife or a pocketbook. In your case, the important thing is the act of selling because you will learn something about customer relations and about a dollar's value. But it's a shame you can't keep the money. If you ask me, it's a scam. Nothing short of child labor."

I knew nothing about child labor, so I didn't respond. A few weeks later I realized he was right about the prize not being the important thing; however, not in the way he thought about it—learning customer relations—no, I learned about people.

"I'll only be doing this a few weeks," I said, wanting him to know I wouldn't be locked into any scheme. As I laid seed packets on his desk, I added, "It's something to do during the winter, and then I'll try for a summer job."

"Good for you. I admire your initiative." He sighed and scowled. "So many young people are far too lazy these days."

With the room so dark and with the antique desk lamp beaming beneath its green-colored glass, I felt like I was in a spy movie where the captured hero must listen to his nemesis outline diabolical plans. The banker unbuttoned his shirt cuffs and rolled up his sleeves. His flabby forearms looked like dough ready for baking. Then he grabbed the liquor bottle from the desk, opened it, and poured an inch into the hexagonal cut-glass tumbler beside it. His drink reflected queerly against his bifocals. "Single malt scotch," he announced. "Richer and smoother than other scotch." He took a sip. "Do you know where this scotch comes from?"

"The liquor store?"

He laughed pretty hard at that. "No, AJ. From Scotland. One thing I've learned is to go to the source. You can't find this scotch in liquor stores here. This particular scotch, which I buy directly, comes from a small, family-owned distillery in Scotland that produces limited batches every year. They still employ many original brewing methods used centuries ago." He put his glass down and grasped the cigar box. "Now, take these cigars, for instance." He opened the walnut box and showed me its treasure. I smelled the earthy odors. "These come straight from Cuba," he said, as if disclosing a federal secret, and then closed the lid. He looked at me, probably waiting for a comment, but I didn't know what to say.

"I see what you mean."

His lips pursed and the moment passed. "So, you're selling seeds."

"I am. And you always have the best-looking place in the neighborhood, so I thought you'd like to buy a few packs."

He grinned. "Flattery. Nice sales pitch." He tapped the desk and leaned closer, and then I smelled his breath, the same stale scent that filled the room. It reminded me of wet paper bags. "AJ, I hire a landscaper to cut grass, trim bushes, and tend flower beds. He does all the manual labor. I don't bother with that drudgery."

"I didn't know that." I began gathering the packets.

"Hold on. I didn't say I wouldn't buy anything. Buying and selling are essential to capitalism." He took another sip of scotch. "Tell me, how are your grades?"

That question, out of the blue, jolted me because my grades had been slipping lately. "They're okay."

"*Okay* isn't good enough." He looked deep and hard at me, and his thick eyeglasses magnified and distorted pupils. He started to speak but stopped. After a moment he said, "I don't have a son; no children at all. Never wanted any. But if I had a son, I'd tell him to get the best grades possible. Do you know why?"

"Getting good grades would mean he's smart."

Mr. Billings waved the back of his hand. "It has nothing to do with being smart. It has everything to do with getting ahead."

"In school?"

"In life." He switched off his desk lamp and slid his chair back. Then he walked to one window and pulled the curtains open; however, the room barely brightened. Being in the house's lower level and facing north, this room rarely saw the sun. "AJ," he said and kept his back to me, "when I was a boy I wasn't popular. I wasn't athletic. I wore glasses and wasn't athletic. Lord knows I was awkward. To be perfectly honest, I was often ridiculed and bullied. Beaten severely a number of times by the bigger and popular boys." He moved to the second window and pulled the curtain back. "But I got good grades. I wasn't the smartest one of the bunch, mind you, but I learned how to get ahead. School—life—it's all the same. You must learn the rules like any other game." He moved to the third and last window and opened the curtain. Even with all three windows exposed, the room was not free from darkness. Perhaps he wanted it that way.

After returning to his chair, he turned the desk lamp on again. "Do you know what good grades do for you?"

"Do?"

He looked exasperated. "Good grades give you options for choosing a college. That's the purpose of high school. Then, a competitive college gives you connections for getting a good job. That's the purpose of college. Do you see?"

I had a hard time looking far enough ahead to picture myself graduating high school let alone graduating college. "Sure."

"Mmm. Tell me, what's your favorite subject?"

"Language Arts."

"English?" A frown filled his round face. "Let me tell you something: Language Arts or English or literature—whatever they call it—is a dead-end. What can you do with that piffle?"

"I'm not sure."

"I am. *Nothing*. Except maybe become a teacher, which means you'll be dining on canned soup five nights a week." He picked up his glass of scotch but only swirled the amber liquid within it. "My wife tells me you've been coming by for art lessons. True?"

I didn't realize she had told him. "Yes. Is that all right?"

"Of course. You're welcome here anytime, AJ. But that's not my point. Devoting time to art is worse than wasting time with English. You won't get anywhere."

"But Mrs. Billings said she's sold some of her paintings."

This made him snort out a laugh. "Yes, I suppose that's true, but it doesn't hurt that I have some wealthy acquaintances with—well, let's say—sympathetic natures. Trust me, selling a few paintings over several years' time will not make you rich."

I was too young to challenge him but also too young to keep quiet. "Maybe I don't want to be rich."

He looked at me as if I'd spoken Chinese. Then he set his glass down and sighed again. When he spoke, it was as if he were saying something he'd told me many times. "In school, physical strength is power, but in the real world, money is power. I came to understand that when I was about your age. My father—well, he was a decent man, I suppose— but he was a failure. He was poor." Now Mr. Billings took a sip of his drink. "Once he tried to pass a check without sufficient funds in his account. His foolish action shamed our family. Because of that, I vowed never to be lacking funds. So, I worked myself into a position of power. In high school I earned strong grades, then I attended a fine university on scholarships, majored in business, established connections, and, upon graduating, secured a good job. From there I worked my way up. All the way to Bank President. Oh, I know we live in a modest town and I might be a big fish in a small pond, but it's *my* pond. Now, the men who come to me for loans are the same type of bumpkins who bullied me as a boy."

I thought of my father arguing with my mother after taking out a second mortgage from Mr. Billings' bank, and how he struggled to make payments.

"No matter what kind of man—educated or uneducated, weak or strong—who enters my bank and wants a loan, must sit across my desk. I can't tell you the pleasure I feel seeing those lowly creatures sweat and grovel." When he hunched over his desk, his bald pate shimmered as it caught a slant of lamplight, and then he held out one hand, palm up, fingers reaching. "I have the power to grant or deny money, the power to grant or deny a better life, the power to grant or deny dreams." He clenched his fingers into a fist and rapped his desk. As his fat body leaned forward, his eyeglasses glinted with the gray winter light. "I have a grand house, a gardener, and a maid. I buy a new Cadillac every three years, and now I have my eye on a Mercedes Benz." Urgently, he leaned toward me and banged the desk again. His voice rose in pitch as his stale breath almost formed a cloud between us. "And I have a gorgeous wife. Ha! I'd like to see any of those brainless dolts match that."

"Maybe," my voice wavered, "maybe we should…"

"So what if she isn't domestic? So what if she pours herself into that idiotic art? Ha! None of that matters. Only one thing matters!"

I sat frozen with eyes wide and mouth open. Beads of sweat had broken across Mr. Billings' forehead. Then, perhaps recognizing the situation and realizing his words, he stopped talking. Fearfully, he glanced around.

After a moment, his emotions were under control. Perhaps he controlled every aspect of his life the same way. In a business-like fashion, he folded his hands on top of his polished desk.

"You have seed packets to sell?"

"Yes, sir," I said, still startled by his transformation.

"I'll take half a dozen."

"That'll be great. Which ones would you like?"

"It doesn't matter. You choose them, AJ."

I set six packets aside and thanked him.

"Don't mention it." He turned to the papers he'd been working on when I'd entered. I stood and waited. Even coughed cautiously. Finally, he looked up. "Yes? Oh, the payment. My wife will take care of that. Just tell her how much we owe."

"All right." I moved to the door but stopped and turned. As the desk lamp glittered on his workspace, ironically it made the rest of the room darker while illuminating his face in a misshapen way. "Don't you want to know how much the packs cost?"

Without looking up he said, "Cost is of no concern."

I made my way to the living room with its oversized windows that let in a lot of afternoon light. Mrs. Billings sat on a sofa, perhaps waiting for me because, when I entered, she sprang to her feet.

"How did it go, AJ?"

Still flustered, I said, "Okay, I guess."

Her left hand reached out and touched my cheek. "My young neighbor and clandestine pupil, there are two types of people in this world, and I'm afraid you and I are of the tender type."

After removing her hand, I still felt the tingle of her touch. I was more confused than ever.

"Did he buy any packets?"

"He asked for six and said that you would pay for them."

She smiled sadly. "Yes, in one way or another, I pay. You see, freedom never comes freely." She reached toward the sofa for a leather pocketbook with long straps. "How much do I owe our traveling salesman?"

"A dollar and a half."

She paid with six silver coins. "A fair price," she murmured and gazed toward the narrow hallway. "No need to walk you to the door?" Susanna Billings turned to me and then looked to the stairs leading to her cloistered world of creation. "You know the way out?"

"Yes, ma'am."

Soon I was outdoors. I stood motionless for a moment and wondered why some people were so pleased with themselves while others were so unhappy.

***

John and Nancy Newcross were in their late twenties and the most physically attractive couple in the neighborhood. John Newcross kept a barbell set in his garage and frequently lifted weights; he swam laps at the YMCA pool, and although he was a successful car salesman, he often rode a bicycle along our streets or into the nearby hills where he pedaled steep climbs and raced down twisting turns.

Nancy Newcross, with her blonde hair, blue eyes, and trim figure, looked like a fashion model. She worked part-time at Enfield's Jewelers although she herself didn't care for adornment. Mrs. Newcross wore only an unpretentious wedding ring and a chain necklace that clasped a small silver cross, which rested against her upper chest.

Their house was a new colonial—second only in prominence to the Billings' opulent home. In summer the Newcross property was a showcase with boxwoods, flower beds, shady trees, and a lush lawn. Nearly year-round, on mornings you could find Mr. Newcross, with intense care, overseeing one part of his landscape.

Everyone knew that Mrs. Newcross tended to the inside of the house; however, she cared for the rose bushes herself and possessed a talent for growing large, beautiful blooms. Also, she was renown for her baking. The neighborhood women especially envied her fruit pies.

In all, they were a perfect couple. John, with his extroverted personality, sandy-red hair, and engaging smile, reminded people of President Kennedy. Sharing the same first name didn't hurt. Nancy was just as charming but not as outgoing, keeping a portion of herself reserved. When the couple first moved into the neighborhood, they hosted parties—everyone was welcome—each Memorial Day and New Year's Day. They'd set out a sumptuous spread of appetizers, meals, drinks, and desserts. But that openness ended two and a half years ago when Nancy suffered her second miscarriage.

I knew Mr. Newcross was home on Saturday mornings and would head to his job in the afternoon. When I approached their house, I wasn't surprised to see him working outside, even though it was winter. He stood by a structure I'd never seen before. After we exchanged greetings, he pointed to it and said, "It's a compost. Built it myself, but I got the idea from Judge Franklin." Mr. Newcross had built a unit that was three feet by five feet. Positioned at its base were two-by-tens and sunk into the ground at the four corners were upright studs. He had attached chicken wire, taut and level, around the whole contraption.

"What's it for?"

He rolled down the sleeves of a heavy-cloth shirt. "Well, AJ, instead of throwing things like coffee grinds, grass clippings, dead leaves, vegetable scraps, and old newspapers in the trash, you toss them in here. Then, every so often, you rake and aerate the pile. Maybe add a little water if it gets too dry. As the stuff breaks down, it turns into a rich fertilizer that I can use in the garden and flower beds. See?"

"I guess so. It sounds good."

"It *is* good. I'll be taking lifeless things and using them to grow other things. It'll be part of a cycle."

I wasn't sure what he meant because nobody I knew did composting then. "Will the compost be better than regular fertilizer?"

"Absolutely. Those big-time companies put so many darned chemicals in their fertilizers, it's ridiculous. Heck, it's dangerous. Everything in *this* compost will be natural. AJ, let me tell you something: you can count on nature, but you can't count on people." He spoke with conviction but suddenly stopped. Then he stared off and something made him wince. After a moment he shifted his feet and focused on me again. "So, AJ, what are you doing out-and-about on a Saturday afternoon? Not cold enough for ice fishing, is it?" he said with a winning smile.

I told him about my flower packets and followed with a compliment. "And you have the best flowers in the neighborhood, so I thought you'd like to buy some seeds."

His face crinkled from a smile into a hearty laugh. "Hey now. A salesman trying to sell a salesman. Say," he snapped his fingers, "maybe we can do a little bartering."

"How?"

"I'll buy flowers from you; you buy a car from me. Deal?" he laughed.

"No deal." I laughed too.

"Well, I suppose you're right. A car isn't the same as a flower. What can you do with a flower but watch it grow?" Then his eyes wandered and he spoke without looking at me. "Knock on the back door, AJ, and have Mrs. Newcross let you in. Talk to her about flowers. I have to caulk some trim before I head to the dealership." He looked at me now and shook his head. "We buy a new house and it's already coming apart." His chin nodded toward the white clapboard and black shutters. "Tell her to get whatever she wants." Vacantly, he stared without moving. Then he pulled a pair of work gloves off his hands and walked away.

About five minutes after I knocked on the black-painted door, Mrs. Newcross opened it. "AJ," she said breathlessly. "I was working upstairs, but I hurried down. Come in." I stepped inside. "You'll have to excuse the way I look. I've been wallpapering!"

She wore an oversized blue and white tattersall shirt that must have been a castoff from her husband. The unbuttoned shirt showed a woman's white tank top beneath. The scoop-neck garment tucked into a pair of dark jeans with glue stains streaked here and there. Her pretty blonde hair framed her perfectly shaped face. I had seen her during their New Year's Day gatherings when she wore make-up, styled hair, and an evening dress, but now, even without those frills, she looked gorgeous.

"Is wallpapering hard to do?"

"It is for me," she said with a chuckle. "Looks like you have something mighty important in that box." Her eyes flashed, perhaps too brightly as she touched the silver crucifix that hung by her collar bones.

"I'm selling packs of flower seeds."

"Is it for a school fundraiser?"

"No." I explained my plan.

"Very admirable," she gently rubbed her hands together. "I was about to glue some strips of paper to a wall, but that can wait. Why don't you go to the dining room and set out some packets on the table? I'm so thirsty, I could use another Coke. Would you like a Coca-Cola?"

In our house we never had Coke, so I was happy to say yes.

Their dining room was spacious enough to accommodate a table with eight chairs, and even a large hutch couldn't fill one wall. The urn-back, wooden chairs had upholstered seats. I sat on a side chair nearest one of the end chairs with armrests and laid out ten different flower packs. Carrying two tall glasses, Mrs. Newcross entered.

"Hold this a minute, AJ. We need coasters." She handed me a drink and from one of the hutch's drawers pulled out two agate coasters with a polished black and white surface on one side and a felt cushion on the other side. "Here you go."

I placed the coaster on the table's glossy surface, thinking how my family didn't have coasters or a hutch or fancy chairs or even a dining room table. She sat on the end chair next to me. I had never been this close to her, and as I looked at the outlines of her flawless face and complexion, I thought of those perfect female characters in Disney animations. But when I studied her eyes, I noticed they were glazed and red. After taking a quick sip of her drink, she took a full swig of it and shut her eyes as if the cola were both powerful and soothing. When her eyes opened, she caught me watching her.

"Oh, the carbonation," she said with embarrassment. "It affects me sometimes. Now, tell me about the flowers."

To know more about the flowers, I'd been reading the packets' backsides and memorizing which ones grew in full sun, partial sun, or shade; which ones bloomed early or late; and which ones needed plenty or hardly any water. I told her just about all I knew, and she seemed interested but I could tell her thoughts drifted a few times.

"People," I said, "have been buying peonies and columbines mostly."

At that moment she seemed far away but then said, "Peonies. We have a bunch of those. I suppose we could try columbines. I should ask John what he thinks."

"He said you should pick whatever you want."

"Oh. Well, I guess it doesn't matter. What else is popular?"

"I've sold coral bells, day lilies, bee balm, soapwort, and bleeding hearts."

She frowned. "Bleeding hearts. Is that so?" She drank more of her Coke, nearly emptying the glass. I wasn't half finished with mine. "No, no bleeding hearts. Coral bells, soapwort, and bee balm. None of them are as nice as roses, but I suppose they'll do."

I heard the back door open, then firm footsteps, then the kitchen faucet turned on and off, and then Mr. Newcross was standing in the dining room. "Did you see any flowers you like?"

"Three or four so far."

He nodded and chugged down half his glass of water. "I guess flowers are one thing we can grow around here."

Her jaws clenched as she spoke through tightened lips. "You should leave soon, John." Then her head tilted back as she drained her drink. "You don't want to be late for work."

"I know," he said and set his wet glass directly on the dining table. "I'll change clothes and put on a face."

After he left, she gripped the table's edge until her knuckles turned white, until her lips flattened against her teeth. It took a full minute, but like a piping tea kettle lifted from a burner, she gradually regulated her emotions.

"Men," she said with a short laugh. Then she found another coaster from the hutch's drawer and slid it under her husband's glass. "They take care of exterior things but are clueless about interior things." She sat down again. "My husband works the three o'clock to closing shift on Saturdays. That's when the dealership sells the most cars."

"It must be fun to sell cars."

"Oh, I don't know. What's a car? Steel and glass and plastic parts—everything designed to be out of date in four years. But take these flowers." She touched a packet. "They're perfect, fragile, and timeless."

"But everyone wants cars. Not everyone wants flowers."

"True. Some people aren't happy with natural things." She must have forgotten her drink was finished because she brought the glass to her lips and angled it high until the ice cubes caught against her lips and water dribbled down her chin. Quickly, she set the glass down, laughed, and wiped her mouth with the back of her hand. "So lady-like." She leaned close to me, her leering eyes inches from mine. "Promise you won't tell anyone that Miss Nancy is not the perfect lady of the realm?"

"Sure," I said and it was then I smelled her breath and realized her drink wasn't just cola. She looked at her glass. "I need a refill. Do you want more Coke?"

"No, thanks. I still have plenty."

I heard her rustling through the kitchen: the clinking of ice, the pouring of liquids. She returned with her face flushed, appearing more attractive because of it.

"You're right about cars, AJ." She sat beside me. "Everybody wants one, and people are never satisfied with what they have. Always moving up." She drank and fingered the cross on her necklace. "When we came here, John drove a Chevrolet; now he drives an Oldsmobile. One day he means to drive a Cadillac. Up, up, up the ladder of success." She chuckled but stopped short when her husband walked in.

He wore a navy two-piece suit—so dark it looked black—a white shirt, and a red-and-white striped tie. He was clean-shaven and smelled of Old Spice, the same aftershave my father used.

"Have we figured out what flowers to buy?"

"Yes, we should have a bumper crop this spring."

"A crop comes in autumn, not spring."

She gripped her glass and stared straight ahead. "Don't forget your overcoat. It will be cold later."

"I know all about cold."

"Should I keep dinner for you?"

"No."

I didn't lift my eyes, avoiding looking at them and wishing I wasn't hearing their tense talk. She took a hard swallow of her drink.

"You should lay off that stuff," her husband said. "Coke isn't good for you." Then he spoke to me in a lighter tone and wagged a finger. "AJ, one day I'm going to sell you a car." Before turning away, he flashed a striking smile.

Nancy Newcross took two deep breaths before taking another drink. Then her breath turned shallow. "Coral bells, soapwort, bee balm, and columbines," she said. "That should do it. One dollar?"

"Yes, ma'am."

"Oh, don't call me 'ma'am'. It makes me feel old."

"All right." I wondered what I should call her and thought she might rise and get the money but didn't, so I grouped the four packs together and put the others inside the cardboard box. After a quiet moment, she looked at me. "AJ, could you spare a half-hour? I could use help with the wallpapering."

"I've never wallpapered."

"You'll only need to hold sheets of paper in place. That's all."

Her eyes fixed on me, this attractive woman with a wounded air, so I followed her upstairs to a corner room. Inside was a baby's crib, a changing station, and a dresser—each painted ivory white. Against two corner windows, white lace curtains hung, curtains that would diffuse any harsh light; the walls were a milky yellow. The room reminded me of a museum display where Plexiglas keeps airless objects preserved.

She pointed to the one wall unbroken by windows where two strips of wallpaper already hung. "I'm only doing this wall because I thought the contrast would help."

I didn't understand what the contrast would help or not help, so I waited for instructions. The wallpaper had a repeating pattern of radiant suns and heavenly colors, which later I learned emulated Hudson Valley paintings.

Absently, she touched her cross again, faced the wall, and whispered, "If I can change this room, I might…" Then she snapped out of her reverie and went to work. "This paper is pre-glued, so we don't need paste, but the hard part comes with matching the images. I should have bought a solid color—no pattern—but I wanted this one. It spoke to me." She blushed. "I guess that sounds silly."

"No, I understand."

She nodded and drank more of her Coke. "We have to dip the paper through this plastic trough and then set the sheet against the wall so the pictures line up perfectly. *Every* line. You'll hold the piece in place while I use this brush to flatten the sheet and glue it to the wall."

She dipped the paper through the trough to moisten the glue, trying to work carefully, but her hands wavered and I wondered if the alcohol might be overtaking the cola. Next, she pinched the sheet's edges and raised the paper to the wall, attempting to find the nexus where everything aligned. Her arms—pale, toned, and lean—fixed the sheet in place.

"Come here, AJ, and hold it now."

My hands switched places with hers as our arms briefly touched. Then she mounted a step-stool and with intent strokes, impelled the paper to stay in place, working her way down. She stepped off the stool, as she whisked the brush past my arms and body, until finally reaching the baseboard.

"You can let go now." She tottered trying to stand straight again. "Good work, AJ."

"What about the pieces above and below the wall?"

"After the glue dries and the paper stiffens, I'll slice off the excess with a razor. The important thing is to line up the pictures." She studied the wall, moving in and back like a human microscope. "Yes, it looks fine, don't you think?"

"I like it."

"Yes, these colors should take away the room's darkness."

"Does the room look dark to you?"

"Of course," she said sharply, then checked herself and rubbed fingers along her thighs. "Didn't mean to bark at you. Sorry."

"That's all right."

"Well now, let's see. Four more sheets should do it."

The next sheet went up as smoothly as the previous one despite the increasing wobble of her balance and the tremor in her hands. Stepping back to examine the work, she seemed pleased but was definitely shaky. After taking another swig of her drink, she grasped the third sheet, lost her footing, staggered, and nearly fell. Regaining herself, she giggled. "Whoa there."

After picking up the fallen piece of wallpaper, she spoke like a child. "Dip the paper into water. It's pre-glued. Hah. There you go, pretty wallpaper." Not only were her words silly, but her speech was slurred.

Holding the paper, she stumbled to the wall and pressed the sheet in place. I hurried to switch places and succeeded without moving the new strip. Mrs. Newcross climbed the two-step stool. "Stay right there, paper, while I brush, brush, brush you into place. Pretty, pretty, beautiful paper. Change my luck. Change my *life*."

Coming off the stool, she missed the step and sailed forward. Her hands slapped the wall, causing the paper to shift. For a moment I froze; then I moved toward her.

"Goddamn it," she groaned, pushed me aside, and frantically pinched and pulled the paper, trying to realign it. As if possessed, she brushed and thrashed the piece into place. Then she reeled backwards, righted herself, limped to the crib, and gripped its upper rail.

I felt helpless. All I could manage was: "Are you all right?"

Breathing hard, she hunched over and nodded. In a few minutes she stood upright and returned to the strip of paper now glued to the wall. Standing close, she examined every inch. Then a cry started in the pit of her stomach—at first a whimper—but it built into a woman's wail. "It's off," she moaned. Her fingers, as if digging dirt from a grave, tried to move the paper, but it was too late. "It doesn't *match*." She fell to her knees.

Then it seemed all spirit escaped her body the way air escapes a punctured tire. She turned so that her back met the wall and then sat on the bare floorboards with her knees bent toward her lips. Her chin quivered and tears dripped onto her cheeks. "It had to be perfect. *Perfect*."

I checked the wall and found where the papers' seams met. Yes, the sheets didn't align, but I could barely tell.

For a full minute Nancy Newcross wept quietly. Then she became calm and her voice steadied. "I've always tried to be perfect. The perfect daughter. The perfect student. Girl Scout, cheerleader. Dean's List in college. The perfect wife. Always, *always* followed the rules." She clutched her head. "And I've *always* stayed close to God. Worshipped Him, gave Him thanks, believed in Him. Asked nothing from Him except…except to have a baby. Just one child. Is that so much?" Her hands opened and her head rolled forward. "I never wanted a career. Even as a girl, all I wanted was to be a wife and mother. That's all. People tell me God has a plan, or they say if something is meant to be, it will happen. But I don't believe that anymore." Now, her fingernails scratched the floor. "I see women—all kinds of women—with flocks of kids. Do they know how lucky they are? I've tried not to be bitter. But I ask, Why is God cruel to me? Oh, I can grow perfect roses. I know how to tend and how to give. There's so much waiting inside of me…waiting to open…waiting to…"

Tears slid down her cheeks, and it hurt to watch her. I sat close, not knowing what to do. Perhaps by instinct, I grasped her hand. Taking two deep breaths, she regained some composure, pulled her hand from mine, and then put both hands around her tucked knees. "I thought if I could change this room—this room that John never enters—if I could change this room, then I could change everything. But how can that happen if John and I don't…we haven't been…." She tilted her face toward me. "So, I've failed again. Don't you see? The lines don't *match*."

"I've looked at the wallpaper," I said as gently as I could, "and the sheets are all right. The lines are really close, so no one will know." Hoping to nudge her out of a darkness, I touched her shoulder, thinking—knowing—I shouldn't, but I wanted her to feel better. She looked at me with sad, sad eyes.

"You're a sweet boy, AJ. Always were. You're different…in a good way." She moved closer. Her beauty overwhelmed me: fair hair, pretty eyes, smooth skin. Even then I realized she would be the most beautiful woman I'd ever know. She murmured, "So sweet and innocent." Then she kissed me, her lips barely grazing mine. Softly, Nancy Newcross pulled back. But without thinking, I returned her kiss. And then she pressed her lips against mine, sending a deep sensation through me. Everything stopped, but my brain was spinning.

Suddenly, she pushed away and shuddered. "Oh, Jesus." She curled into a ball and whispered, "Oh God, what am I doing?"

I couldn't speak or move.

After soundless minutes, she wiped her face with both hands and straightened her shoulders. She did not look at me. "Thanks for you help, AJ, but I'll hang that last sheet of wallpaper myself." She stood and steadied herself. "And…and of course, the seed packets. I promised to buy four. One dollar, right?"

"Yes." I wanted to say more; I wanted to run off; I wanted to stay.

"Go downstairs and I'll meet you by the back door."

I had done something wrong, something terribly wrong. As I walked away, my stomach tied into knots.

While I stood by the back door, she returned, looking calm and attractive. "Here you are." She handed me a dollar bill.

"Mrs. Newcross…I'm sorry…I…"

"No, AJ. *Nothing* happened." She gripped my shoulders as if waking someone from a troubled dream. Her expression was grave. "You helped me hang wallpaper. I bought seeds. And that's all. Okay?"

I nodded.

"All right, then. Go on home and say hello to your folks."

I stepped outside. As the door closed, I saw Nancy Newcross's young and lovely face vanish as another one—old and pallid—appeared.

FIVE

After leaving the Newcross house, I should have headed home, but I was too rattled. Where could I go? I thought of walking to the town center, going to the Vesta Diner, and ordering a hot chocolate. I pictured myself alone in one of the restaurant's big booths with its burgundy vinyl seats and tufted backs. It would be warm there and, although I was an infrequent customer, the waitresses— older women—were nice to me, the same women who sassed working men who ate weekday meals there. But it was easy to tell that the men enjoyed the rough banter more than they enjoyed the food. During the summer I sometimes rode my bike there, and one day a waitress called me "cutie-pie," and the name stuck. That led to all the waitresses giving me a free slice of pie whenever the owner, Ernie, wasn't looking. But winter was no time for biking, and walking wouldn't make sense because I couldn't get there and back before sundown.

During the summer, I could go to the ballfields, sit in the bleachers, and watch men play in softball leagues.

Along with a range of ages, there was a range of talent, which made for some funny moments: bobbled balls, terrible slides, and screwy strikeouts. Most men took a relaxed attitude toward the games, but some were fanatical. In order to win, they coaxed, implored, or threatened their teammates.

During the summer I could go to Moccasin Pond and its encompassing, primal woods. It was a true pond, spanning no more than one hundred feet in length and width. Depending on rainfall, its surface was either murky or glassy, but it was always a favorite place for flocks of mallards. Winding through the forest, as old as the original Native American tribes, were trails of leaf-strewn, soft earth. I loved wandering the paths, being lost in a world of variegated greens, yet it was autumn's colors that dazzled me most, along with the season's pungent scents that signaled the shifting of nature's cycle. I loved autumn, even though it flourished with decay. I could live for the dying. But hiking to the pond and trekking through snow on a winter's day would be foolish.

I moved along, perhaps subconsciously aware of the warm place, and the only place, I could go: Our Lady of Lourdes Church. It was a half-mile away, north up a hill for two streets, and then west one block onto Central Avenue. It was a suburban church with middle-class houses flanking its property. The building's cornerstone showed 1953, so it was new, as far as churches go, and it was nothing like the older city churches with their dark pews and stained-glass—so much of it that sunlight barely trespassed. Our Lady of Lourdes pews were white-washed oak, the hymn books and kneeling pads were tanned leather, and the windows were completely clear. The lectern was the same oak as the pews and behind it, centered, was a life-size cross with an impaled Savior; the cross and Jesus were made of clear pine. The twelve-inch square floor tiles were white with tan streaks. And no smell of incense imbued the air. Later on, I seldom stepped inside a house of worship, but on the day I left Mrs. Newcross, this church took me in.

The front door was never locked, so I entered the pristine place. Not a priest nor a parishioner was there. I walked down the center aisle and sat in the third pew. However silent I tried to be, my smallest movement caused an echo. Soon, I felt warm enough to slip off my jacket and gloves, but the image of Nancy Newcross leaning toward me and the sensation of her lips on mine lingered. I didn't feel at ease and wondered why the incident had happened. Was it my fault?

I tried to pray and to find forgiveness. Although it had been awhile, I thought of seeking a formal confession, but how would I tell a priest—either Father Michael or Father Timothy—what I'd done? I remembered sitting in a shrouded confessional and the sudden, quick opening of the priest's portal; the whispered words; the penance afterwards. Then I remembered taking the Eucharist—the body of Christ— every Sunday Mass and kneeling at the altar, waiting for Father Michael to make his way along the penitents. He'd hover by each of us and say something in Latin. I remembered tilting my head back. The old priest would place the sacred wafer on my tongue firmly, as if it were a postage stamp. All the while an altar boy held a burnished salver beneath my chin, so if the Eucharist slipped past my lips, it wouldn't fall to the floor. I remembered my father taking me to Mass every Sunday, yet I sensed he never wanted to go. For the past several years, we had attended less frequently.

I sat for at least fifteen minutes in a pew and hoped to witness a heavenly sign, or better yet, to hear a celestial voice echo through the church, absolving me of all sins. But no sign or sound came.

When another ten minutes passed, I mustered a defense for my actions. Nancy Newcross was exceptionally beautiful, and, after all, it takes two people to make that kind of mistake. Still, I wanted to make tangible amends; however, the only idea that came to me was to light a candle. I had seen people do that. But why? To remember their dead? To wish for something?

I walked down a side aisle that led to a table of votive candles—the glass blood-red—as it is in nearly every church. I realized people slipped coins through the slot of a black metal box attached to the table, a small price for dispensation. Then I remembered the twenty-five cent piece that Mrs. Warren had given me, and I remembered her wish. Of course, her coin had merged with the others inside my zippered pouch, but dipping my fingers into that pouch, it was easy to pretend I'd picked her coin out from the rest. Without truly understanding, somehow I knew that Mrs. Warren's wish could connect to Mrs. Newcross.

After dropping the coin through the slot, I lit a candle and watched the solitary flame flicker against the crimson glass. Watching the tiny light glow and dance, I said a prayer for Nancy Newcross but wished nothing for myself.

Outside, after I buttoned my jacket and tugged on gloves, I headed home and, despite the darkness, felt relieved.

***

"What the hell have you been doing, AJ?"

"Sorry, Dad."

"'Sorry' doesn't change anything." My father's left hand held my report card as the back of his right hand slapped it once.

In those days, especially within a small school district, the teacher handed each student his or her report card in a sealed manilla envelope and each student was expected to take it home, have it signed by a parent, and return it to the teacher. When I came home that afternoon, after handing the card to my mother and after she scanned my grades, she placed the envelope on the kitchen counter exactly where she had placed the delinquent bills weeks before.

Without a trace of emotion she said, "Go to your room and wait until your father comes home."

Now he was home. He wore a twill shirt, unbuttoned and untucked. Layered beneath it was a stained undershirt. Even beneath his clothes, his chest and arms were defined.

"I didn't realize my grades were so bad."

"D's in math, science, and social studies?"

"I have a 'B' in language arts."

"Right."

"And my grades in gym and…"

"AJ, I don't give a rat's ass about gym or music or art. It's the important subjects that count. What the hell have you been doing?"

The answer was obvious and of course he knew it, but *I* had to say it. "I've been selling flower packets after school every afternoon."

"And then you come home, eat dinner, and are too tired for school work. Right?"

"I guess so."

"I know so."

He set the report card on my dresser and faced me. His fingers squeezed into fists and then loosened again. I feared he would hit me, but he had never hit me. I didn't know what to expect, still I was surprised when he sat on the opposite side of the bed from me. His hands rested on his knees and he stared at them. Then he rubbed his cheeks and chin as if wiping away water. His face sagged with an expression I had not seen before. He looked tired, but deeper than tired; he looked sad, but deeper than sad.

"AJ, do you think I like working in a factory?"

I didn't expect the question and wasn't sure how to answer. "I don't know."

"Do you think I like standing on a cement floor all day in a noisy, smelly, shitty place? Cold in winter, hot in summer. Taking a half-hour lunch in a ten-by-ten room buried in a basement. Do you think I like that?"

He had never talked to me about his job, let alone described it. "I guess not."

"Would *you* like it?"

"No."

"Good, because only a dumbbell would say yes." He tried to smile, but it wouldn't come. "That's why you need good grades. You learn things in school so you can go to college where you learn more things. I never had the chance. Having a college degree gives you options. So instead of settling for a job, you can choose a career. You won't be stuck in some god-awful factory. You won't have to work a half-day on Saturdays to help pay bills. You understand?"

He looked at me with his deep-set eyes that always seemed as if they were sifting grain from chaff. "Yes," I said, because unlike Mr. Billings' scenario, my father's made sense.

Then he slid off the bed and stood to his full height. "So, what do we do now, about your grades?"

"I don't know. Maybe it's too late?"

"These are progress grades, not semester grades, right?"

"Right."

"So, it's simple. You make up every assignment, and I don't care if it's for full credit, half credit, or no credit. You make up every last one. Understood? Because it's not just about the grades. Okay?"

"Okay."

"And you have to work double-time to keep up with your current assignments."

"But."

"No buts." My father had regained himself. He was strong and sure. "So, you know what this means. After school you come straight home. Have a snack maybe. Then, it's straight to your room and hit the books. No going out, no selling flower packets. No nothing until you're not only caught up, but ahead. Clear?"

"Yes."

"AJ, if you don't do this…"

His chest expanded and his chin jutted forward, but he didn't finish. I don't know if he couldn't find the words or if he couldn't say them. Either way, when he left the room, I trembled, not because of fear but because I started seeing my father in a new light.

***

For two weeks I stayed in the house after school to catch up on class work, so I couldn't sell a thing. To boost my grade, some teachers offered extra assignments. I should have been more thankful. Confined to my room, I worked hard—mostly. Now and then I'd look through packets and read about each flower or I'd flip through the prize catalog and study the paint set or I'd count my sales and calculate how many more I'd need to reach my goal. But beyond those things, something else was forming, some insight. I realized I liked being in other people's homes. Some moments were tense or strange while other moments were calm and common, but sitting in my room, I missed all of it, the good and the bad. And I realized that because I knew how to be quiet and how to listen, while inside those intimate settings, it was as if I became invisible and some people opened themselves. So much so, I imagined that most of what they revealed to me, had never been revealed before. So, briefly, I was a part of their lives, and yet I was always apart from their lives. Perhaps that is how most artists function. As I turned away from people, I turned people into my art.

One Saturday, after finishing my schoolwork—I finally had caught up or close enough— I thought it safe to sell again. My father was home and napping after working an overtime shift and my mother was in her bedroom with the door closed, so it was easy to slip away.

The afternoon was clear but cold, so I didn't want to walk far from home. Across the street from Our Lady of Lourdes Church, two priests, along with a domestic, lived in a spooky-looking house. Being a Victorian style home in need of repair and complete with gingerbread, narrow windows, lattice, and a wraparound porch, the neighborhood kids christened the place haunted. I didn't believe in ghosts, but while walking up those creaky porch stairs and clutching my cardboard box and leather pouch, I felt more than edgy. And I pictured the priests with their black garments, secret knowledge, and singular lives. They were mysterious beings. Not as mysterious as nuns, but still, there was something foreboding about them. Also, because they were close to God, I wondered if the eerie house might possess some heavenly power that held sway over visitors.

When the door opened, Miss Hooper the housekeeper, appeared wearing an ankle-length calico skirt, a pink blouse, and an amused expression. She was an elderly, waif-like woman: tiny, thin, and angular, most notably her chin. She pushed aside a lock of gray hair from her green eyes and pointed a bent finger at me. "With that peddlin' box under ya arm," she said with a thick brogue, "ya wouldn't be some young capitalist fixin' to bamboozle me now, would ya?" Her twinkling eyes belied her stern words.

"Oh no, Miss Hooper." I quickly explained why I was there and what I hoped to do.

She nodded. "Father Michael might have an ear for you, but I don't know as young Father Timothy has much concern for flowers. He spends a world of time reading the Bible or the newspaper or one of them old books from the shelves, which he would do well to thank me for dusting."

I tried to make my case. "Every year the priests have a flower garden."

"Right ya are, AJ. But have ya noticed how poorly it's been lookin' for such a time?"

I told her, yes, because I *had* noticed.

"To tell truth, for years and years Father Michael tended the garden. He'd be at it near every morning. Loved it, he did. But now he struggles. He's got the gout and rheumatiz' and Lord knows what else. Why, ya'd think some neighbors would pitch in and till the earth—if only they thought their kind acts would later transport 'em to heaven." She looked upward with a shrewd laugh. "Only Mr. Carter, good man that he is, has come by the last three years to give Christian aid, but he can only do so much, what with his own home and family. It saddens me heart to see Father Michael scrabble in the garden after all these years, and…and…" Miss Hooper's eyes watered. Embarrassed, she blinked away tears and changed her tone. "Now then, AJ, ya want to addle some brass?"

"What?"

She smiled. "Ya want to earn some money?"

"If it's okay."

"'Tis well. Step into the foyer here and wait. The both of me masters are sitting in their study thinking their deep thoughts. I'll ask if they'll grant ya an audience." She winked.

I sidestepped Miss Hooper, who stood to my brow, and after she left I surveyed the foyer but was disappointed because it lacked any supernatural signs. The walls were papered a sea-green, broken by vertical white stripes. The floor's pine planks were dark, and a faded Oriental rug covered most of the area. In the corner was a coat stand with a pocketed base that held one tartan plaid umbrella and two black ones.

Miss Hooper returned. "Ya may scoot yourself in," she said and waved her hand so I would follow her down the hall.

We came to a sturdy, eight-paneled oak door as dark as the floorboards. The housekeeper grasped the antique knob and pushed the portal open. Both she and door groaned. Inside, the room was as shadowy as a secret.

"Why, hello there, AJ," Father Michael, the priest I'd known all my life, greeted me. "Do you know Father Timothy?" He nodded toward his counterpart.

The two men were similar in that they wore black shirts beneath black sweaters and each man wore a pair of black trousers, but their differences were great. For one thing, age separated them. Father Michael's once-dark hair was now mostly white. His face was wizened, his stomach wide, his shoulders bowed, and he grimaced as he stood up. Father Timothy, on the other hand, had flaming red hair and a burst of freckles on his smooth-shaven, boyish face. He was tall and lanky with a bounce to his limbs as he stood.

"I've seen Father Timothy," I said, "but we haven't met."

"And now we meet," he said and shook my hand with a firmer grip than I'd expected.

"If there's nothin' else," Miss Hooper interjected, "I'll be fixin' dinner."

"Thank you," said Father Michael. "And what will dinner be tonight?"

"It will be whatever it is I fix." The elderly woman emphatically raised her pointed chin and made her exit.

After she shut the door I realized just how dark the room was. Thick wool curtains covered all the windows' thin glass. The wallpaper was an earthy brown with a repeating shape similar to an amber coronet. Wooden shelves lined two walls and held hundreds of books, apparently the ones that Miss Hooper dutifully dusted. Two lamps, unlit, stood on two pedestal tray tables. The priests sat on identical club chairs upholstered in a royal red cloth, and the men angled themselves toward the cramped fireplace where several logs burned and offered orange rays and scant warmth; standing just a few feet from the fire, I felt the room's chill while flames highlighted each man's face.

"What's this I hear?" Father Michael began, "you're selling flowers?"

"No, Father, I'm selling flower seeds. Packs of them." I pulled two from the box and showed him. Then I explained my situation.

Father Timothy said, "I admire your entrepreneurial spirit."

I must have looked confused because Father Michael said, "He means you're a go-getter."

"Oh."

"AJ," Father Michael began with a sigh, "I loved tending flowers, but I'm seventy-seven years now and a wee weary, so you see, my gardening days are a step behind me." He spoke with a shortness of breath, but his fleshy lips formed his words perfectly. His dark eyes were piercing, and I thought he must have been a handsome young man. "I don't believe Father Timothy has tended flowers. Am I right, Father?"

"I'm afraid that's true."

"But allay your fears, lad." Father Michael spoke with a lilt in his voice, not as thick as Miss Hooper's but pleasant just the same. "We'll help a parishioner in need. What do you say, Tim? Should we purchase some flowers?"

"Indeed we should." Father Timothy nodded firmly as his blue eyes glistened from the fire's glow.

"Bring that chair up to the fire, AJ." The old priest pointed to a square table across the room with three Shaker-style chairs tucked under the table's legs.

I placed my chair between the two priests. Being closer to the fireplace, I felt warmer, so I slipped off my jacket and hung it on the chair's crosspiece. From the box I pulled more packets and handed a few to each clergyman. "The back of each package," I explained, "tells about the flower. How to plant it and what it needs."

"It couldn't be that flowers need sunlight and rain," Father Timothy said slyly.

"Sounds like an allegory." Father Michael winked. "Perhaps I may use it in a sermon?"

"We reap what we sow?"

"Aye, too true." To face me more, he shifted in his seat and murmured, "Oh, these ancient bones."

"Have you taken your pills?"

"Aye. Too many pills. I'm tired of pills." He looked squarely at me. "Tell me, AJ, are you keeping up with your studies, with your school work?"

I felt a lump in my throat and wondered if priests really had the power to peer inside people's souls. "Well, I fell behind a little, but I'm caught up now."

"That's good; however, you mustn't fall behind. Education is important; I know because it's something I lacked for years." He hesitated, then spoke again. "I was born in Ireland but know nothing about my parents. You see, I grew up in an orphanage, which at the time was no better than a county prison. Every day felt like a full year. When I was twelve, I ran away and found work in the bogs, in the peat fields. Grueling, backbreaking labor." His eyes and lips tapered as if reliving some brutish memory. "After two years of that, I purchased a one-way fare to America. You see, a priest in the local countryside often helped young lads emigrate to America. His kindness impacted me greatly. Father Peter, he was. A man built like a stone stable but with a heart like a nurse-marm. He saved my life."

The three of us sat quietly for a moment, weighing the older priest's words and staring at the fire that flickered and flashed and steadily diminished; it needed more wood, and for that purpose a small pile of split logs and chipped kindling braced by the hearth. Breaking the silence, Father Timothy said, "My grandfather came from Ireland, too. He was a farmer of middling means. But when he came to America, he landed in New York City; no place for a farmer, so he turned to bricklaying."

"Hard work."

"Yes." The young priest's eyes locked onto the fire and perhaps he, too, saw distant images. "My grandfather had four children; the youngest being my father. He wasn't one for bricks, so he started painting houses. Outside and inside. The man grew his business from nothing. Scraped and scratched and saved. Heaven knows how he did it. But, a tough-minded man can shape the world to his dreams, I suppose. I remember him telling me that people will always need their homes painted, so it was steady work. Eventually, his two older brothers joined him and the business grew even more. They're all doing well, financially."

"Most vocations heed to money. Maybe folks who take the other roads are called noble hearts."

"Or naive fools."

"Aye, it seems money is more important to people than ever." Father Michael shook his head. "Many folks have turned away from the spiritual world, from spiritual needs." He regarded the young priest. "Each year we lose more parishioners."

"True. Old folks die off and young folks don't join."

"And what's worse, we're losing the middle group." The old priest shook himself, straightened his shoulders, and spoke with passion. "For decades the church played a central role in people's lives, not just births, weddings, and funerals. We sustained community, what with raffles and dances, picnics and socials, pancake breakfasts and spaghetti dinners, catechism classes, clothing drives, and food drives. But most important, we were the Word of the Lord. Not only Sunday Mass but daily Mass as well." He stopped, took a breath, and composed himself. Then he looked at me. "I've noticed you and your father don't attend Mass as often as you once did."

"My father," I thought to say, "works a lot and sometimes he's really tired on Sundays."

"I see. I expect it takes a world of strength to sit through a one hour service, does it now?"

"No, Father."

"Would it harm you both to make a more regular appearance?"

"No, Father," I said, not knowing that in a few weeks no one in my family would attend church again.

Two burning logs crumbled as the fire began collapsing onto itself, choking itself, but neither priest stirred to place new wood on the dying flames.

"Father," the young priest said, "you've told me how you came to the priesthood, but will you tell the story again? Perhaps for our young friend's benefit?"

"Happy to oblige." The man turned to me. "So, it was Father Peter who planted the seed within me although it took time for it to bloom. Yes, Father Peter was the first person to treat me kindly, and I never forgot what one man could do for another. You needn't be rich or powerful, just compassionate. So, this humble man of the cloth made a grand impression on me." Father Michael locked his hands together and rested them on his broad stomach. "When I reached America, Boston that is, few gainful opportunities there were for a lad of fourteen, but I found a job with that great newspaper the *Boston Globe*. At that time they hired young fellas to do heavy work, and after toiling in the peat fields, I was muscle-ready. So, I was put with an older fella who drove a newspaper van. I hauled stacks and stacks of papers from the lorry to newsstands, but it was easier than spading muddy earth." He lightly pinched one earlobe and tucked his hands together again.

"Then came the Great War. That's what they called it, or The War to End All Wars. Well, as with so many advertisements, it proved itself malarky. Now, because of my flat feet, I wasn't eligible, so I watched a generation go off to die, or worse. It was during that time, gradually, my life became as clear as crystal and I knew I must do something to heal mankind, especially those who had been wounded, and, by the saints, not by war only. So, I wrote to Father Peter, you see. I knew that one lad he'd helped to America became a priest.

"Sure enough, through Father Peter I learned that the lad—now a man—headed a seminary. Through this connection, I applied for and was accepted into that seminary. There I found my first formal education. And I found my calling." He sighed. "Aye, Father Peter twice aided the course of my life. Ever since, I've been trying to do the same for others."

The three of us stared vacantly at the dying fire, and I wondered if I should rise and place a piece of wood on the fading flames, but Father Michael coughed quietly and said, "And you, Tim. I've asked twice before about your journey to the priesthood, but you've only given me hazy accounts. Will you tell the tale now?"

"Yes. And indeed my account might be labeled a 'tale.'" The young priest slide back in his seat. "I was an awkward boy. Never good at studies and never good at sports. Even after my growth spurt, my body never caught up with itself. I was forever clumsy and lacked confidence, which made all social situations dreadful for me. Besides that, I had no natural talent for *anything*. No matter what I tried, I failed. So, I didn't fit anywhere. Due to all that, I learned to keep my own company.

"After graduating college with a liberal arts degree, I was suited for nothing. The worst of it was, I couldn't light on a career because nothing appealed to me, especially the painting business. I thought of being a teacher, but I wasn't sociable enough. In fact, I wanted a permanent hiding place. So, eventually, I worked it out in my mind that I should become a priest."

"But, Tim," Father Michael looked at the young man with a start.

He held a hand up. "I know, Father. It's the worst possible reason."

"It is indeed."

"I'm ashamed to say it." He paused and gathered himself. "But then, fortunately, in the seminary everything changed."

"Everything?"

"Yes. Halfway through seminary I was still adrift and thought I could continue drifting. But one winter evening, I had the strangest experience. After supper, I felt tired but restless, so I went for a walk. The seminary grounds were beautiful, especially one meadow surrounded by a forest. I walked to the farthest point, to a tree that was detached from the forest about twenty yards onto the meadow. It was a sycamore tree, solitary and lonely. I reached it and—for no reason at all—put my hand against it, touching its bark. It was cold yet alive. With my great coat pulled round me and a tweed cap upon my head, I sat on the ground with my back against the tree.

"It was one of those gray winter afternoons when the sky, earth, and forest form endless shades of shadows. Suddenly, I felt terribly tired, on the verge of sleep. So, I closed my eyes for a good while, and when I finally opened them, winter was gone! Spring had blossomed in every corner of my sight. The sun glowed warm and gentle with a golden nimbus crowning its circumference. The sky was pale blue, the grass a Lincoln green, and the trees were budding pink and white.

"I wondered if, like Rip Van Winkle, I had somehow fallen into an enchanted sleep and now awakened. In amazement I gazed around, wanted to stand, but couldn't. Something held me fast. Before me lay a world of beauty that I couldn't reach. It seemed everything I wanted was at hand; however, I was tethered to the ground. I didn't know what to do. So, I closed my eyes again, waited a good while, opened them, and found that winter had returned: the gray, the chill, and the darkness. Awed and frightened, I jumped to my feet and hurried away."

"What on earth or in heaven," asked Father Michael, "did you make of it, Tim?"

A silent spell passed before Father Timothy, staring into the sinking fire, answered. "I still struggle with the whole of it." He bowed his head. "But I believe God sent me a sign. A miraculous sign. I had been wasting my life by living in shadows, and I knew that another world—a wondrous and celestial one—was waiting for me if only I would move toward it. And I knew people were turning away from the Light. And so, I decided it was my duty—my calling—to revive God's Spirit."

The old priest solemnly shook his head. "That, my lad, is a glorious tale."

"Yes. But, Father, do you think it's a true tale?"

"I think you've spoken truth. Do you doubt my belief in you?'

"Not at all. No, I doubt *my* belief in the vision's reality. With no one else as a witness, I cannot say it actually happened. Perhaps I was in some sort of intermediate state of existence. As when you're about to write a sermon and a marvelous idea seizes you and takes shape in your mind and you sense inspiration—Divine Inspiration. And then you go to write it out. You write, yes, but the words fall short. Reality, or your own skills, prove poor. Our imagination exceeds reality. So it may be with my vision. Did I dream the entire thing?" The young man scowled. "And after wearing these black garments for such a time, I wonder if a priest has any power at all. Can words make a vision come true?"

"Such a question."

The room grew dimmer as the fire waned, yet neither priest rustled.

Father Timothy leaned forward as if searching for something. "I'm twenty-seven years old and I've been in the service of our Lord for three years, but I don't know that I've made one bit of difference. The sermons I've crafted often center on loving one another, which works well in the pews, but when parishioners leave this sheltered place, they turn to their natural habits: a law of the jungle and a me-first philosophy. It starts with gathering grand possessions, and it ends with coveting trivial things. Why, I've seen people battle over parking spaces—in our own lot. So, what good have I done?"

Father Michael's head drooped. "After all the years, I ask myself the same question."

"From what I can tell," the young priest said with hands on his knees, "there are two groups of people. First, the ones who are doing well and think if they continue to worship Jesus, they will to continue to prosper. Then the others who are not doing well—the poor. They relate to Jesus' suffering because it comforts them. Fine. But the shame of it is, neither group looks to the other. Neither group reaches out to the other. So, what have I accomplished?"

"Hoping to accommodate shifting times," Father Michael stated, "the Church has changed, but the changes come from people's weaknesses."

The priests spoke contrapuntally in bleak tones—surely forgetting I was there—and for many minutes I only heard voices in the dark.

"Folks want the Mass spoken in English, not Latin."

"In Latin or in English, we still lose people."

"They don't want to kneel anymore."

"An inconvenience."

"An hour's time for Mass is too demanding."

"A loosening of mores."

"A dearth of decorum."

"A splintering of commonality."

"The family unit unravels."

"The community frays."

"A divided country."

"Rich versus poor."

"Black versus white."

"Man versus woman."

"*The center cannot hold.*"

"And what slouches toward us?

"A terrible future."

"An apocalypse?

"No, not the end of times. Survival, but with dark days and darker nights."

"What can be done against the Immanent Will?"

"Nothing. So, what have all my years wrought?"

"And how shall I last half as long?"

"With the state of things and with the state of my body," Father Michael sighed, "God forgive me, but death would render welcomed relief."

As the three of us slumped in our seats and stared at nothing, the fire dwindled to a few crimson embers, and a palpable dread filled the room like incense at a funeral Mass. The priests' exchange made me shiver, and I wondered if this moment held the rightful meaning of "haunted" because it contained true horror—horror not confined to a house possessed.

I wanted to say something to fill the emptiness, but if my father had taught me anything, it was to know my place. So, I waited. I waited until time itself may have stopped. Finally, I cleared my throat.

"Oh, AJ," Father Michael said. "Indeed, you're here. And your packs of lovely flowers. Yes, yes, we will surely buy some." The old priest tried to stand but sank back in his chair. "Ow," he growled painfully. Then he looked up, perplexed. "Lad, buying seeds is easy, but nurturing a garden is hard. Who will set the seeds and tend the soil?"

Silently, we sat for awhile. Then, like a specter, Father Timothy stood, stepped toward the fire, but stumbled. He righted himself, picked up two pieces of kindling and tossed them onto the embers. He leaned close to the coals and blew a long, hard breath onto them. Like a conjured spirit, an amber flame leaped, stretched, and curled around the new wood. Without a word, the young priest returned to his chair.

SIX

Before entering the Novello house, I stood on top of four brick steps that led to the front door and smelled something delicious. The evening had turned colder as I walked from the priests' house to the Novello home and the chill from their study stayed with me, so when Mr. Novello opened the door and waved me in, I didn't hesitate. Inside, a landing balanced between two short sets of stairs: one going down and one going up. Standing there, I felt a little wobbly, not only because I didn't know whether to go up or down, but because I was hungry and the savory smell and snug warmth made me feel as if I could melt like a tiny marshmallow in a mug of hot chocolate.

"Upstairs, AJ," Mr. Novello said with a laugh.

The man was about five feet six inches tall with a lean, strong body. In his early fifties, his short, straight hair was dark and his beard stubble was thick. He had a smile that made you smile. I don't know if he ever stopped smiling for long—perhaps long enough to laugh—and when he laughed, his whole face burst into merriment like a benevolent sovereign of an untroubled land.

"This type of house is called a raised ranch," he said. "Not a big house, but every square foot is usable space. Me, I'm the kind of guy who likes to get his nickel's worth."

We climbed six stairs to the upper level. To our right was a hallway and to our left a square living room that formed an "L" to a dining room. Straight ahead was the kitchen and by the doorless entry stood Eleanor Novello, an impressive woman of width and height, standing three inches taller and probably weighing twenty pounds more than her husband. Although a stout woman, she had a handsome face. Over her housedress she wore a smudged apron, and her broad smile suggested nothing but happiness.

"AJ, are you here to sell flower seeds?"

"How did you know?"

"Nothing happens in this neighborhood," she said with a laugh, "that I don't know about."

"What's this about flowers?" her husband asked.

I told Mr. Novello my enterprise. He smiled, put a hand on my shoulder, and walked me inside the kitchen, which was also a square space and not much larger than our kitchen, but here at least were plenty of storage cabinets. The most striking difference, however, was the fragrance of homemade food. Across from us, another archway opened to the dining room. Attached to the kitchen's corner walls were benches flanking a rectangular table. Behind each bench hung a framed print of Jesus. One featured a detail of his face in profile with a halo crowning his golden-brown hair. The other showed him sitting upright on a rustic bench with lambs and children by his feet. Boys and girls gazed up in wonder as He spoke.

From one cabinet Mr. Novello fetched a wine glass and set it on the table. A festive bottle of red wine followed. With his head hanging low, he poured a full glass and then looked aslant at me with a mischievous grin. "Do you like wine, AJ?"

He laughed and his wife said cheerfully, "Eddie, the only wine that boy will drink will be during a church Mass." She turned to the stove where two pots simmered: one with pasta, the other with marinara sauce. Then she opened the oven to check a pan of baking meatballs.

"Ellie, why are you always so proper?"

"Because one of us has to be."

Then his face brightened. "Wait. I know a time when you slipped up. Remember Mrs. Murphy?"

His wife rolled her eyes. "Not that old joke."

"Hey, don't spoil it." He looked at me, his face glowing. "Once my wife told me that Mr. Murphy kisses his wife goodbye every morning. Then Ellie asked me why I never do the same. I told her I would, but I didn't think Mr. Murphy would like it."

He broke into a hearty laugh while his wife laughed just as hard. "I tell myself not to laugh at his silly jokes," she said, "but I fall for them every time."

"Let's face it, I have a way with words."

"Okay. Now, how about having a way with the table? Like setting it. And put out a place for AJ. You'll have supper with us, AJ?"

In fact, I was hungry, and the food smelled fantastic. "Maybe I could call my parents and let them know?"

"Use the phone," Mr. Novello cocked his thumb to the yellow Bell Tel hanging on the wall. "Leave a dime on the counter."

"Eddie!"

"All right, all right. No charge. And then you'll help me set the table." He hung his head with exaggerated gloom. "Ugh, I'm reduced to women's work."

"I'll take care of that, Daddy." From the hallway, Teresa, their older daughter, appeared. She looked like a younger version of her mother, nearly the same height, dark brown hair, and plump but attractive in a full-bodied way.

Her father grinned. "Ah hah! The calvary has arrived."

"Hello, AJ." Teresa's voice was soft and pleasant. "Do you remember me?"

"Sure, but it's been awhile." I calculated Teresa must be in her mid-twenties.

"Time flies, doesn't it? But you were always a cute kid and that hasn't changed." She smiled warmly. Embarrassed, I bowed my head.

"So," Mr. Novello said, "call your parents and let Teresa know if she's setting an extra place."

The phone call was brief. My mother seemed unconcerned that I wasn't coming home or when I'd return.

"Let's go to the living room, AJ." Mr. Novello held his glass in one hand, grasped the bottle of wine in the other, and stepped toward his escape.

In this room, the furniture—coffee table and end tables—were dark but piebald with ivory-colored, crocheted doilies. The sofa and chairs were big-boned colonial pieces with protective fabric over the armrests. I looked into the dining room as Teresa set placemats and silverware, and I noticed two built-in china closets in each corner. They were painted an off-white to match the walls.

"Those china closets are beautiful."

"You like those? Yeah, I built them after we moved in."

"Really?" The cabinets had fluted frames and a sheet of glass revealed the top shelf just below a crescent peak. "They're terrific."

"It took some time, but I thought it was the best use of space. Like the kitchen table. Ellie wanted a round table, but I built a straight one that fit in the corners. I built the benches, too. More practical." He drank a good portion of his wine. "Now, the girls are too big for those benches, but the set-up worked for years."

"Where did you learn to build things?"

"By trying. Sometimes that's the only way." I thought of my art work and how Mrs. Billings gave me the chance to try. "And I've always been good with my hands," he added. "For years I worked construction, building houses mostly."

"You don't do that now?"

"No. See, I never owned a construction business; always worked for someone. So, instead of taking a day off to dodge the winter cold or summer heat, I worked through all kinds of weather. It gets to your bones."

"That must have been hard."

"Yeah." He drank more wine and refilled his glass. "So, two years ago a friend of mine, Vito, got me a job in the factory where he works. It's noisy as hell and I'm still on my feet a lot, but I don't have to deal with bad weather."

"I guess, overall, it's better?"

He tilted his head in a philosophical manner. "I don't know, AJ. I'll tell you something. After working in a factory for awhile, I think it's an unnatural place. See, people weren't made for places like that. We don't belong there. Yeah, working outside can be tough, but you learn to get along with nature and all its ways. And you're closer to God."

"But some work has to be done indoors."

"Right. White-collar jobs, I guess. As long as you can hear yourself think. You can't have a hundred machines howling around you." He grinned. "Hey, do you know what we make in my factory?"

"No."

"Benches." He nodded to reassure me. "The benches you see in all the parks? We build them. Yeah. Ninety-nine percent of our work is for the state, but sometimes individual costumers pay for a bench and have it placed in a public park, and they have a plaque attached to the rest-rails with a dedication to a departed loved one. You know," he raised his right hand as if tracing the words, "in memory of so-and-so who did such-and-such." He smiled. "Well, I figure when I go, I'll have a bench made with a plaque, too. 'In Memory of Eddie Novello, One Helluva of a Great Guy.' Then below that in big, big letters: KEEP OFF!" We both laughed at that one. Then, he clapped his hands and said, "Now, let's see those flowers."

I laid ten packs on the sofa and while he examined them and muttered thoughtful sounds, I felt completely at ease. Even though the sun was close to setting, the house was full of light. Each lamp in that room—four of them—glowed, and five tapered bulbs in an ornate fixture hanging over the dining table shimmered; a warm golden light streamed from the kitchen. Rising above everything—including occasional cooking clatter—was Mrs. Novello's unrestrained, cheerful humming. She didn't follow a fixed melody but instead created a song that belongs to every strong woman.

"I like these four," Mr. Novello said and separated the packs from the others. "How much did you say they were? Ten cents apiece?" He gave me his sidelong look again, and I knew he was kidding.

"That was last week's price. This week: twenty-five cents."

"For the love of gravy," he chuckled, "why didn't you stop by last week?"

"Well, I…"

"Too late, too late. Looks like I'm stuck." He pulled a wallet from his back pocket, and we made the exchange.

"Hey, Eddie," his wife poked her head out from the kitchen. "È ora di mangiare."

"Yes, ma'am. On the double, captain." He stood. "Hey, where's Regina?"

"I'll get her, Daddy." Teresa turned to the hallway.

I was finding my place at the table when the younger daughter appeared. In height and build, Regina clearly took after her father's lean body, but she had light brown hair, and her face favored her mother's pretty features—how Mrs. Novello might have looked when she was her daughter's age, which was twenty. With her eyes fixed straight ahead, not noticing me, Regina spoke with a quick, no-nonsense cadence.

"I have a big-time history exam next week and that rambling professor, well, his lectures are impossible to follow, so to be safe, I'm going through the textbook page by page. Oh. Hello, AJ. What are you doing here?"

"Regina!"

"Sorry, Mom."

Her father said, "He's selling flower seeds."

"Oh. Are we on a bartering basis now? Flowers for food?"

"Regina," Mrs. Novello said with exasperation.

In a sing-song voice, she answered, "Sorry, sorry, sorry." Then she giggled. "Just pulling your leg, AJ."

Mother and father sat at opposite heads of the table. I sat across from Regina and between Mr. Novello and Teresa.

Mrs. Novello said, "Teresa, please say Grace."

The family grasped hands and I felt a bit awkward as my fingers touched two outstretched hands. But I did what was expected. Mr. Novello's hand, calloused, felt as rough as a steel file. I could only imagine the hours of labor it took to earn those marks. Teresa's hand, however soft, still carried traces of toil.

"Oh, Lord," she began, "thank you for the food we are about to receive. Thank you for keeping this family in good health. We pray you keep watch over all people, great and small. And thank you for letting us share this meal with one of our neighbors. Amen." We echoed the word and with a tender squeeze, Teresa released my hand.

Never before or since has a meal overwhelmed me with such aroma and flavor. In a maternal way, Teresa piled spaghetti onto a Corelle plate with its decorative green trim. Then from a gravy boat she ladled pools of tomato sauce over the pasta. From a third serving dish, she plopped two meatballs, each nearly the size of baseballs, onto the plate and handed it to me. From a small bowl, the family spooned grated Parmesan over their food, so I followed suit. The Parmesan's scent was so strong that I tasted the cheese before it passed my lips. To finish the medley of food, a plate of Italian garlic bread made its way around the table.

Carefully, I stirred my fork into the spaghetti and twirled the strands into mouth-sized chunks. As I chewed and swallowed, I nearly moaned with delight because the pasta I knew—what my mother cooked— always reminded me of plastic spindles, but this spaghetti was soft and fresh. And unlike my mother's sauce that came from a can, this sauce was rich and spicy. And the meatballs by themselves were enough to make a meal.

For several minutes I didn't raise my head but ate determinedly, moving from pasta to meatballs to bread, stopping only to wash things down with a gulp of water. Then suddenly, somehow, I felt everyone's eyes on me. I looked up and saw their amused smiles. Flustered, I dropped my fork onto the plate. "Sorry," I mumbled. "I didn't know I was so hungry. Or that the food was so good."

Regina laughed. "Better not barter for flowers, Pop. We'll need a greenhouse to grow them all."

"Pay her no mind," Mr. Novello said with a smile. "You're supposed to eat, so *eat*." My cheeks burned. "And another thing, we all have wine except you. Here," he grabbed the wine bottle and poured some into my water glass. "Not full strength but enough to taste the grapes."

"Eddie," Mrs. Novello chided, "his parents might not want him to drink that."

"Because they're not here, we don't know if that's one hundred percent true. So, there's a fifty-fifty chance."

"But, Eddie, he may not like it."

"AJ, take a drink so we can let the jury rest."

After sipping cautiously, I found both spirit and flesh willing. "It's pretty good."

He laughed and turned a forkful of pasta against a spoon. "Wine is what Jesus drank. At *every* supper. Not just his last."

"Another meatball, AJ?" Teresa asked, and before I could answer, she spooned one onto my plate.

"Such a mama-pajama this sister of mine."

"Oh hush, Gina. Go study your college books."

I listened to the banter between sisters, which was only good-natured teasing.

"I will. But you should save some of that lovey-dovey stuff for Mr. Reynolds."

Teresa blushed. "I hope you're right."

"AJ," Regina looked at me, "did you know Terri made the meatballs and the sauce?"

"No."

"She did. And let me tell you, neither is easy to make."

"Gina, I'm sure AJ isn't interested in my cooking."

"Maybe not, but I like to brag on you now and then. AJ, I bet you didn't know that Terri was the first in our family to graduate college."

"A *community* college."

"Whatever," Regina waved her hand. "Then, with no help and no connections, she landed a job with the Jefferson County School District as a secretary to James P. Reynolds. Outstanding, wouldn't you say?"

"Sure," I answered, not knowing anything about James P. Reynolds.

With a confidential nod, their mother chimed in. "A marriage engagement might come this summer. And soon, who knows," she looked to her elder daughter, "grandchildren?"

Teresa raised her hands. "Now, take it easy. You're putting the cart before the horse."

Mr. Novello's face filled with a smile. "Don't worry. We're only saying you might be married soon. And that reminds me of a story I heard at Clancy's Bar the other night." The three women grumbled with stage effect, but that only made him more intent. "A police officer called in a crime to his desk sergeant. He said, 'A woman shot her husband for stepping on a floor she had just mopped.' The sergeant asked, 'Have you arrested her yet?' The cop said, 'No, not yet. The floor's still wet.'" Laughter from Mr. Novello; grousing from the women.

We resumed eating and with the watered wine and magnificent meal, I felt full and content. Even the garlic bread, with its crunchy crust and textured center—so different from the Wonder Bread my mother tossed onto a side plate—was delicious.

As we were finishing, Teresa asked her sister: "How difficult will your history exam be?"

"Definitely challenging because, although the prof is brilliant, he just can't teach." Regina dangled a fork over her plate. "But I understand the textbook. It's well-written, so I'll be all right."

She possessed a certainty that could not be second-guessed.

"Can I help you study your notes?" her sister asked. "I could say a topic, and you can tell me what you remember."

"That's a great idea. Thanks, Terri."

"Have to keep you on track." She smiled and turned to me. "My sister is on her way to becoming a lawyer."

Now Regina turned modest. "Oh, I'm not even halfway there. I have a l*ooo*ng way to go."

"But you're *on* that road," her sister said proudly. "Not many women dare to take it."

"This daughter of mine will be one heck of a lawyer," her father stated. "Hey, that reminds me of another story I heard at Clancy's. I think it's a true story." Undeterred by another chorus of groans, he continued. "It seems that the devil stopped into a young lawyer's office late one night. He said to the young man: 'I have an offer for you. If you give me your soul and the souls of everyone in your family, I'll make you a full partner before the month is through.' The lawyer pushed his chair back and studied the devil for a full minute. Then he said, 'What's the catch?'"

After two silent beats, the table broke into laughter. Then Regina said, "Hey, I'll be an *honest* lawyer, Pop."

"Of course you will," her mother assured.

"Yeah, I know," Mr. Novello said, but then, for the first time, a shadow touched his face. "You girls know we don't have a pot of gold. Your mother and I scrimped and saved and set aside enough money to get you both through college. With Teresa going to a community college, we have enough to pay for one year of law school. But after that…" He held up his hands as if they were scales. "I just don't know."

"Don't worry, Pop, I'll make it work." Regina grasped her father's hand. "I'll find a way. But what worries me is trying to make it in 'a man's world.'" She released her father's hand and looked straight ahead. "Well, I don't want the world, just a piece of it. But most men don't take women seriously. A woman's brain is her only body part that men never measure."

"Regina!"

"It's true, Mom. And I don't know if that will ever change."

"Maybe with women like you, Gina, things *will* change."

"I hope you're right, Sis, but men have power and they don't want to lose it. They want to keep the status quo."

Mrs. Novello said, "You must keep praying to God, and things will work out."

"Of course, Mom, but I can't just sit on my hams. God helps those who help themselves."

No one spoke for awhile as we finished our meal. The tangible elements before us—pasta, meat, bread, and wine—decreased, but the intangible elements— love, warmth, kindness, and light—increased.

Finally, when Teresa asked if she could take my plate, I was so entranced, I didn't want to ruffle my waking dream. But I couldn't eat another bite, and I knew my time with this family had ended. Reluctantly, I lifted my plate. As Teresa grasped it, she smiled radiantly. I forced my chair from the table and braced myself to leave.

***

A few months back, on Saturday nights my father started making dinner, but with a twist. He cooked breakfast: eggs, bacon, oatmeal, and toast. After working a half day at the factory and doing chores around the house, somehow he found the energy to make our meal. I'm not sure why he did this, and I don't know if my mother liked or disliked the idea, but it was impressive to see him orchestrate the food so everything was ready at the same time, especially the eggs because mine were scrambled, my mother's were over-easy, and his were sunny-side up.

We were finishing the meal when my father stretched his arms and yawned. Even though the house felt chilly as usual, he wore slacks and a short-sleeve T-shirt. Maybe he didn't feel the cold like I did. "Knicks play the Celtics tonight," he said, perhaps trying to peak my interest or to give himself a reason to spend the next two hours in the family room. He carried his plate to the sink, set a stopper in the drain, ran cold water to fill the basin, and said, "We'll let the dishes soak." He reached for my plate. I handed it to him but stayed at the table. Then he opened the fridge and checked inside. "Need a fresh six-pack," he said and headed to the back porch.

During the fall, winter, and early spring he kept two or three packs of beer on the porch where they would stay cold and not take up room in the refrigerator. At that moment my mother's shoulders arched like an animal's preparing for an attack. My father returned holding in one hand a six-pack of beer and in the other hand a plastic ashtray with one cigarette smoked to its butt. After setting the beer on the counter, he lowered the ashtray toward my mother, who had eaten little of her meal.

In a stern voice he said, "You told me you quit smoking."

"That's what I said."

"Looks like you didn't quit." He slammed the ashtray on the counter.

"That cigarette," my mother said apathetically, "has probably been there for months."

"And I never noticed it?"

"That's my guess."

"I put beer on that porch every three weeks, and I grab a six pack from that porch every week, and I *never* saw that cigarette? How does that happen?"

"How should I know?"

"Look, all I know is, I never saw this cigarette until now."

His hands balled into fists as veins along his throat bulged. I thought it perverse that, as his anger heightened, her tone lowered, and I wondered if my mother had purposely left her cigarette in the ashtray.

"So you said," she stated without emotion. "I'm not arguing with you."

"But you *are* lying."

"Am I?"

He stepped toward the table. I stood up. "It's me," I said. "*I* smoked it."

"Is that so?"

I nodded.

"Hell, I bet you don't even know the brand." He took the butt from the ashtray and checked the print on the paper.

"Lucky Strike," I said, remembering what my mother smoked.

"Where did you get it?"

"From a girl at school. Linda."

"Why?"

"I just wanted to try one." I shrugged. "I know some kids who smoke all the time."

My father sat at the table across from me. "So, what did you think? Did you like it?"

After waiting long enough to seem that I thought about it, I said, "No."

"Good." He glanced around the kitchen and then concentrated on me. "AJ, you're getting older and temptations are out there. I can't keep you from smoking cigarettes. But I can tell you they're absolutely worthless. Nothing more than cancer sticks. And dying of lung cancer is a miserable way to go. Coughing, spitting, wheezing. It's more pain than a person deserves. You hear?"

"Once was enough for me," I said as innocently as possible. "Never again."

"I hope so." He turned to my mother. "I'm sorry. I guess you did quit."

"You see." A queer half-smile came to her as she picked up a slice of toast and spread butter on it.

My father pulled a beer from the six pack, placed it on the counter, and put the other cans in the fridge. "Game's already started," he said and headed for the family room.

For her toast, my mother knifed another slab of butter and spread it so thick, I cringed. Because I had somehow saved her, I stared at her, wanting her to look at me, wanting a word or a sign. Nothing came. She just ate her toast. Enjoying it so much, she didn't notice the disgusting smear across her lip.

***

The days passed slowly, but the weeks went fast. At least, that's how it felt. Late March: afternoons grew longer, days turned milder, and dogwoods budded pink or white. My sales were doing fine, but I needed to send everything in by April 14, so I kept at it in order to reach my goal.

I told myself not to stop at the Carter house because I didn't know them well. I wondered how would they see me, trying to sell them something without a personal connection. But I had stopped at many other homes without knowing the owners well, and something Miss

Hooper had said about Mr. Carter stayed with me, his helping Father Michael with the flower garden. Still, I was reluctant to ring their doorbell. The Carters were Black. The only Black family in our neighborhood.

Their ranch-style home was built before the second world war. The original owners were a retired couple; however, when they turned quite old, they neglected the house, so it fell into partial ruin. Before moving to a nursing home, they sold the place to the Carters, and now the house and grounds looked perfect. The roof shingles had been replaced, the siding scraped and painted, the asphalt driveway resealed, and the grounds were lush and symmetrically landscaped, but not to where the growth overwhelmed the property. The most impressive part of it was that Mr. Carter had done all the work himself. No hired hands and no neighborly help.

Mr. Carter answered the door but opened it only a few inches. He wore oxblood leather slippers, pressed gray pants that would pair with a suit jacket, a white dress shirt, and a sweater vest. When I started to introduce myself, he raised a hand.

"Yes, yes, AJ, I know who you are. Is anything wrong? Any trouble?"

I said no and told him why I was there.

He had short-cropped, natural hair and a mustache two shades darker than his skin. He cocked his head as if calculating something. "So, you come all the way here just to sell me flower seeds?"

"When I visited the priests, I saw Miss Hooper and she said you've helped Father Michael with gardening, so I thought you might want to buy seeds for your own garden."

"Uh, huh. When I can get 'em at the hardware store across the street from where I work?" Disbelief came to his face, but I didn't look away. He frowned and a look of resignation followed. "I reckon I'll *have* to buy some. I can hear them loose tongues flappin' how the Black family didn't buy even one pack from that poor white boy. A cryin' shame. Only they wouldn't say it so nice."

My face turned red. "If you don't want to buy any seeds, that's okay. I'll go and won't tell anyone I was here."

His eyes fastened onto mine, mine onto his. Then he laughed. "Aw, man. My bark is worse than my bite. Only take half of what I say as gospel. The other half is Mother-wit." He smiled, opened the door wide, and waved his hand. "Come on in, AJ. It's still winter out there."

Linoleum covered the three-by-six entryway, which opened to the living room. Like all the old ranches, this was the house's largest room with the largest window. Stepping into that room, was like walking onto a family TV show from the late 1950s. A beige wall-to-wall carpet covered the floor. A camelback sofa and wingback chairs showed a Colonial Williamsburg influence. The end tables and coffee table were Queen Anne and darkly stained. On the coffee table, neatly arranged, were magazines: *Time*, *Life*, the *Atlantic*, and the *New Yorker*. Wainscoting flanked a squatty brick fireplace. Above the wainscoting were built-in shelves filled with hardbound books, and walls were painted a rich, creamy yellow. Hanging on the walls were handsomely framed prints of Americana moments: Washington crossing the Delaware, the Signing of the Declaration, and others.

"Been a long day," he said and sank into the wingback chair close to the fireplace and motioned for me to sit in the matching chair. "Being a bank teller puts me on my feet near all day. Know what I mean?"

"Sure, I understand."

"Mmm." He looked at me the way my father looked at me. "Well, maybe." From his sweater pocket he pulled a pack of filterless Camel cigarettes. He clicked open a silver lighter and flicked the gear that produced a flame, its glow weak against the two lit lamps, yet the room was dim because the lamps were fixed to a low setting and the sun was waning.

As he lit the cigarette, Mr. Carter's brown eyes squinted, his distended nose widened, his mouth sucked in smoke and blew it out. He studied the Camel cigarette and said, "This here is the one vice I have. Smoking. Well, a man's entitled to one vice, right?" He puffed the cigarette and then laughed softly. "My wife would say I have more than one vice—many more." He tapped the ashes into a glass ashtray. "So, you been talkin' to Miss Hooper?"

"When I went to the priests' house, she answered the door."

"Yeah, that's right. Nice lady." He worked his cigarette. "How 'bout them priests? Buy anything?"

"They bought four packs."

His eyebrows rose. "That right? I'd like to know who's gonna plant them seeds."

"I'm not sure."

"Yeah, right. That young priest don't know nuthin' 'bout plantin' nuthin'. And Father Michael, well, I don't think he's up for any more plantin' seasons. So, I reckon that leaves me."

Then, sounding like a small explosion, I heard the back door bang open, followed by pounding feet, laughter, and a playful voice crying out: "You are going to get yours!"

A boy about six years old sprinted into the room and when he saw us, skidded to a stop. Another boy, probably two years older, rounded the corner and skidded to the same stop. Their mouths hung open as their eyes darted in every direction. Mr. Carter stood up and glared. The boys didn't—or couldn't—move.

Then Mrs. Carter entered the room from the opposite end. Her manner projected complete control. Severely, she crossed her arms and spoke in a firm, composed voice. "Thomas Carter and Jonathan Carter, is that the way you enter this house, or anyone's house?"

"No, ma'am," the boys said as one.

"Especially with a guest in the living room?"

"Sorry," they said and hung their heads.

For the first time, Mrs. Carter looked at me. "You'll have to excuse our boys, AJ. Sometimes they don't know what to do with their energy." She uncrossed her arms and stood benignly, wearing a blue blouse and white slacks. She was a trim, statuesque woman. Her hair had been straightened and cut in a style that reminded me of Jacqueline Kennedy's.

"That's all right," I said and wondered if I should stand, too.

"I know what they can do with they energy," their father said in a clipped voice. "They can do homework, and after that, they best be readin' a book."

"You're absolutely right, but first they can help me in the kitchen. I'm making Yankee pot roast with mashed potatoes, carrots, corn, and biscuits. I need potatoes peeled and carrots sliced." She looked at her sons with eyes as sharp as arrowheads. "Understood?"

"Yes, ma'am."

"All right, then. *March*."

The boys silently headed to the kitchen. She waited until they were gone before smiling and winking at her husband who returned the smile.

"AJ," she said in a warm voice, "you're welcome to stay for dinner, but it will take awhile."

"Thanks, Mrs. Carter, but I can't stay tonight."

"There's always next time." Gracefully, she moved to the kitchen.

Mr. Carter sat down, snubbed out his half-smoked cigarette and pulled out a second one. He looked at it, frowned, and laid it on the end table. He spoke with agitation. "It's one thing for boys to be boys—and I don't want them to be nothin' but boys—but they have to learn actin' like that won't get 'em anywhere. No, sir. They must be proper at all times." He picked up the cigarette and firmly tapped its end on the table. "And they *will* do good in school. Get good grades. No wastin' time with football or basketball. If they have to play something, it'll be the piano or violin or something like that." With finality he said, "They goin' to dress right, sound right, and *be* right."

After pinching his cigarette, he lit it and smoked deliberately, sitting rigidly for a few minutes. Soon he relaxed and spoke calmly. "AJ, there's a lot of unrest in this country. I know certain changes will happen, but I also know what a Black man's gotta do to get ahead. You understand?"

He was asking rhetorically, but I didn't know it then. And I certainly didn't know what his life was like. Indeed, I knew little of the outside world, gleaning secondhand experience through TV news. I was a suburban product who lived in a papier-mâché world, but because of my recent door-to-door outings, I was discovering the "quiet desperation" of my neighbors, and I was beginning to understand the disquiet of my own home.

"I think so."

"Mmm, maybe." He tilted his head back and seemed to savor the inhalation of cigarette smoke. Then he straightened himself. "But anyway, let's have a look at them flower packs."

Relieved to take them out, I grabbed a bunch and handed them over. Even though the room was darker now, he didn't click the lamps to a brighter setting. I wasn't sure if he could see the packs clearly, but I thought maybe he was used to seeing things through a different type of darkness.

"From what Miss Hooper says, you know your flowers."

"Among other things." He laughed softly again, and it was within his gentle laughter that I believe the true Mr. Carter existed. "Let's see here." He held the packs like a poker hand. "I definitely could use some columbine." He set a packet to his right. "Can't use no sunflowers. They grow too big. Need a field for them things. Now, Shasta daisies would be nice. And morning glories."

"Mrs. Billings chose a pack of those."

"That right?"

I nodded.

"You know, all the years I been workin' for Mr. Billings at the bank, I never met Mrs. Billings. I know she keeps to herself mostly, but I also know Mr. Billings has had gatherings at his house."

"They live next door to us, so I see Mrs. Billings a lot. She's nice."

"I'm sure she is, but that's not my point." He placed two packs of morning glories and one pack of Shasta daisies with the columbine. "You said these were a quarter apiece?"

"Yes."

"No five-for-a-dollar deal?" He grinned.

I smiled but told him no. He extinguished his second cigarette before it was finished.

"The wife tells me to quit smokin' but that's harder to do than climbin' a greased pole, so I been goin' halfway with my smokes."

"Sounds like a good plan."

Just then a burst of laughter echoed from the kitchen. Mother and sons joined together. Whatever scoldings Mrs. Carter had issued must have expired somewhere between potato peeling and carrot slicing.

"But one thing to know," Mr. Carter said, picked up the flower packs, and shuffled through them, "is that morning glories don't grow like regular flowers. They need something to grip on to. They got some vine in they veins."

"Could they grow up along a mailbox post?"

"Yeah, they could. Say, that's a fine idea, AJ. That way, when the mailman come by in the mornin', he'll have something pretty to look at."

"He should like that."

"Well," he stretched his arms and then reached to a pants pocket and pulled out his wallet. The black bifold was worn and scarred, as if it had been in battle. "Looks like I owe you this." Lifting a dollar from the wallet's folds, he handed it to me.

"Thanks, Mr. Carter."

He looked surprised and then hurt. "You know something, of all the people that come and go at the bank and for all the years I worked there, your father is one of the few who calls me Mister Carter. Everyone else calls me Horace. For a fact, the other men tellers get called Mister; the women tellers get Miss or Missus. Course, they all white."

He tapped another Camel against the end table before putting it in his mouth. After lighting it, he pulled on it twice.

"Say, that reminds me. Do you know the Smith sisters?"

"Kind of. They live on the other side of the neighborhood."

"That's right. Now let me tell you, AJ, before you get out of the seed sellin' business, you oughta visit them. Bet you'll make a sale. Hey" his expression brightened, "you got time for a story?"

"Sure."

"Know how I got hired at the bank?"

"No, sir."

"Okay, years ago they had a teller job open and I applied. I didn't have all the credentials or the experience, but I had the belief—the grit—I could do the job. When I applied, Miss Myra Smith had been workin' at the bank a long while. You know, she worked her way up to all kinds of positions. By then she was the one readin' the applications and doin' the interviews. Then she'd send two or three folks on to Mr. Billings to do the hirin'."

"Did she send you on to Mr. Billings?"

"You jumpin' way ahead." He drew on his cigarette and as a smile creased his face. "No, Mr. Billings never spoke to me." He shook his head. "When I walked into the bank for the interview, you shoulda seen the look on folks' faces, but Miss Smith treated me like a complete person. Interviewed me like I was worth something. Toward the end of our talk, I asked her why she interviewed me. She said when she was a girl she had a friend named Isabelle Carter who bragged she was a descendent of the Carters with a big ole plantation years back way down in Virginia. Miss Smith asked me if my family come from there, too. I said I didn't know. But I do know that wasn't her reason for hirin' me at all."

My curiosity grew. "If you weren't sent on to Mr. Billings, how did you get the job?"

He laughed. "Miss Smith hired me herself. Right there." He nodded as if still surprised. "See, Mr. Billings was out of town on vacation. Miss Smith was supposed to send folks on to him the following week, but she told me to start tomorrow. And I did. By the time Billings come back, shoot, it wouldn't look right for him to undo the deed."

I remembered Mr. Billings' study and how every object had its place. "I bet he was sore."

"I 'spect he was and I know he watched me close for the first month or two, but I worked hard and I worked right so he had no reason to fire me." Mr. Carter set his cigarette, still burning, in the ashtray. "Never figured out why Miss Smith did what she done because she must'a caught a good deal of grief from Mr. Billings, but, you know, there's something unusual about that woman. She's gentle but strong. And maybe she understands what it's like to be on the outside lookin' in.

I don't know. Anyway, she stuck her neck out and went against the grain, and for that I'll always be grateful."

"Dad?" Two voices sounded. Contritely, his sons stood at the room's edge. "We're finished in the kitchen, and we'll do our homework now."

He stretched a hand toward them. "Come here, boys." They came up and he introduced us. Then he said, "What's the homework tonight?"

Thomas, the older one, said, "Math."

Jonathan said his was Reading.

"Both are important subjects, boys. Very important."

"Yes, sir."

"Later, after you finish and after we eat, me and your mother will check your work."

Thomas flashed a smile. "Like always?"

"Yeah," his father chuckled, "like always." He looked at me. "I check their math and Esther checks their English." Then he glanced at the flower packs. "Hey, boys, look at these flowers."

His sons grasped the packets and gazed at them. Jonathan said, "They sure are pretty."

Thomas said, "What are they for?"

"For plantin' outside the house. Now, some flowers are annuals; they bloom once. Yes sir, one and done. But some flowers are perennials; they go on and on."

"Forever?"

"Close enough. Yeah, some flowers come back every year. They survive. Even though they get beaten down by rain, snow, and hail, they pull through. Gotta be tough."

"Resilient." Thomas said.

"Now that's a ten dollar word!"

"It's from last week's vocabulary."

"Hey, it's got the right meaning, and that's what it takes: resilience. Now," he rubbed his hands together, "guess whose job it's goin' to be to plant them flowers and tend them? *Yours.* Both of you. Plant 'em right and give 'em enough water and pull out any weed before it gets ideas. Keep an eye on the annuals but keep an extra eye on the perennials."

"But, Dad," Jonathan said, "I don't have an extra eye."

Mr. Carter laughed and with a son on either side of him, he clasped their shoulders. "Me and your mother love you dearly." He gave each one a swift swat on his backside and sent them off. The boys laughed, started to run, but stopped, probably recalling their latest episode.

I sat and tried to remember if my father had ever said those words to me.

Mr. Carter reached for his cigarette but let it burn. "Some folks might say I'm too hard on my boys. What do you think, AJ?"

"I don't think so."

"Mmm. Like I said, life for us is different. But if my sons go about things the right way, they *will* succeed. Yes?" He looked at me with eyes that seemed to want reassurance, but I wasn't the person to ask.

"Of course."

He looked relieved. "Sometimes I think about the future and believe nothin' will change. That my sons will face the same hateful eyes I faced. That gets me down." He moved to the edge of his seat. Now the room was steeped, not in darkness but in shadows as the lamps glimmered. He raised his eyes like a man searching the night sky for starlight. "But then I think of the sacrifices people have made and the strides. And when I think of folks like Dr. King and maybe them Kennedy brothers, I have hope." He reached for his cigarette, but it had turned to ashes.

We sat quietly for awhile, and then I said, "I should be going."

"Reckon it's time." Mr. Carter stood and turned his head. "Esther," he called, "our guest is leaving."

Although Mrs. Carter was deep in preparing dinner, she entered the room looking as regal as she had looked before. "Thank you for stopping by, AJ. Next time I hope you can stay."

"This one here," he wagged a thumb at his wife, "is a fine cook."

She stood close to her husband. They definitely looked like a married couple; in fact, they looked like a painting. Standing a few feet from them, I tried to interpret their expressions. They didn't look fearful, yet they didn't look fearless. I would say, committed.

"Maybe I can stay for dinner soon."

"That would be nice. In the meantime, say hello to your parents," Mrs. Carter said before turning toward the kitchen.

Mr. Carter walked me to the front door. "Where to next, AJ?"

"I'm not sure."

We stood and faced each other. "Now, from here it's a hike, but you should stop in on the Smith sisters. "Don't wait," he said with a tender laugh, "because they both in their seventies. Now, let me tell you, Miss Jenny is a might ornery, but Miss Myra is as sweet as pecan pie."

SEVEN

After leaving the Carter home, I did not call on the Smith sisters, who lived farther away; I kept them for another afternoon. Instead, I walked to Miss Sarah Wells's house because, although we knew each other as distant neighbors, I was more than a little curious about her. She taught high school English, and her reputation as a popular, caring teacher filtered down to my grade level. And it was possible I'd be her student in the fall.

Built before World War II, hers was the smallest house in the neighborhood, and its simple floor-plan could have been created by a child. The front door opened immediately to a living room on the left and a dining room on the right. Together, the rooms wouldn't equal the size of the Billings' family room. Adjacent to the dining room was a galley kitchen with few cabinets, scant counter space, a sink, a stove, and a refrigerator, all of which consumed most of the room. Ten straight steps from the entry door down a tight hallway was the main bedroom on the left, and three steps beyond that was the lone bathroom and a tiny second bedroom to the right. No upstairs, no basement.

It didn't take long for Miss Wells to answer the door or for me to tell her why I was there. "AJ," she said with a laugh, "when it comes to gardening, I'm all thumbs, and not one of them is green."

As far as making a sale, I was disappointed; however, beyond that, there was something captivating about Sarah Wells, and I sensed no sadness or anger within her, as I had with Mrs. Newcross or Mrs. Warren.

"Have you tried to grow flowers before?"

"Um, not really."

I gave her my most forlorn expression.

"All right, all right," she raised her hands and smiled so broadly that her big brown eyes squinted and lines by her lips revealed traces of past smiles. "I will not turn away a soon-to-be student of Washington High School. Come along."

"Thanks," I said, and as she held the front door open, I slipped past her slim but feminine figure and nearly brushed against her pink, cabled sweater that fit tightly over a white blouse.

I stayed close behind her as we walked to the second bedroom, admiring her long brunette hair with its strawberry highlights and the olive-green slacks that clung to her shapely legs. No, she was not as beautiful as Mrs. Newcross or as bohemian as Mrs. Billings, but Miss Wells was special in a different way.

We stepped into the small second bedroom that had no bed. Two white bifold-doors concealed a closet; two four-drawer filing cabinets stood like watchmen; and one glider window, spanning three feet high and four feet wide, allowed natural light to fill the space. The walls were an off-white and the floorboards were three-inch-wide oak strips stained honey-gold. An old-fashioned desk by a swivel chair was the room's focal point.

"I've never seen a desk like this."

"They aren't common today." She touched the blemished surface of a leather insert. "It's called a partner's desk. They were popular in the 1800s, and I think they originated in England for bank executives. It's designed so that two people can work on it at the same time. Here, sit down." She pointed to the opposite side from where she would sit.

I pulled out a ladder-back chair with a rush bottom, but the seat was piled with paperback books that toppled to the floor. "Whoa," I called out.

"Oops," she said with a laugh. "AJ, when I'm not looking, some brazen books climb onto that chair. Happens all the time."

"Your books can climb?" I asked with a grin.

She smiled a Ferris wheel smile. "Of course, but only when my back is turned."

Miss Wells snatched some fallen books—Hawthorne, Shakespeare, Dickinson, Twain—and plopped them on top of a filing cabinet. I did the same.

"I'm afraid that chair isn't very comfortable. I've been meaning to find a seat cushion for it."

"That's all right." I sat and felt just how uncomfortable it was, but the desk between us was fabulous. The mahogany wood showed marks where people had worked. Within reach, was a blue pottery bowl filled with paperclips, and lying on the desk's surface was a stash of red pens.

"The desk and this chair," she grasped the wooden armrests of her green leather chair, "my father bought at an estate sale years ago. He was a school administrator and my mother was a high school English teacher."

"Like you."

"Yes, although *I'm* like *her*." Her pretty eyes danced. "My father sat in this chair and my mother sat where you are, but in a much nicer chair. They often worked together. It gave them a chance to know each other in different ways. It's one thing to relax together, but by working together—even if you're working on separate tasks—you learn a person's layers. They were quite close."

"Do they still work like that?"

"No," she pursed her lips. "No, they've both passed on. Both too young."

It felt like a rock dropped to the bottom of my stomach. "I'm sorry."

"So am I." She glanced out the window and then at school papers piled on her desk. "I positioned the desk here," she said, "because this room faces west. The sunlight, you know?"

"Sure."

"As you can see, I have plenty of grading to do, but I'm making progress. Almost finished with this essay." She held up two stapled sheets of composition paper. "Then I'll need more coffee, and we'll talk about flower seeds. I could fix you something. Hot chocolate?"

"That would be great if it's not any trouble."

She laughed. "AJ, the coffee is freeze-dried and the cocoa comes in packets. The only thing I do is boil water."

Miss Wells turned to the essay and grasped a Bic pen. Almost every kid in school used Bic pens because they were cheap. I remembered how Mr. Billings wrote with a fancy fountain pen. Now, this English teacher worked through a student's essay, sometimes nodding her head in approval and writing a notation in the left-hand margin or sometimes frowning and writing a notation in the right-hand margin. I liked watching her reactions because they were easy to interpret. And I liked her pretty face. Her wide brow tapered gradually to a firm chin. Her high cheekbones kept a natural rosy color, her complexion was smooth and flawless, and her brown eyes gleamed with intensity while she worked through the composition, as if lost in a special dimension as she considered the student's handwritten words.

After reading the complete essay, without hesitation, she wrote a note to the student and then set that composition on top of others, which I took to be her "finished" pile.

"In-class essays," her cheeks puffed and then released a breath, "are challenging. Students can't use notes or check sources, and with the clock ticking, it adds extra tension. Their essays amount to a rough draft, so their work isn't the best, but a teacher must allow for that."

"What are they writing about?"

"Success." She smiled. "They have to define success as it relates to *The Great Gatsby*." She must have noted my blank expression. "It's a novel. A fine one, too. AJ, do you like to read?"

"Yes."

"Good. Keep at it because reading and writing are the heart and soul of education. They're the foundation for *everything*. Do you know what I mean?"

"Sure."

That made her laugh again. "I hope so, but something tells me you're buttering me up to make a sale."

"Oh, no. I…"

"Don't worry, AJ, I'm an easy mark. Yup, a teacher makes a defenseless target during the school year with one fundraiser after another, so I'm constantly buying things I don't really want or need. It's part of the job." She looked past me with satisfaction. "No, I shouldn't call teaching a job. I wouldn't even call it a career. It's really a lifestyle. Actually, the classroom side of things is just the iceberg's tip. People don't know the grading time or the preparation time or the meeting time." Her words held no trace of complaint. In fact, she sounded grateful. "And the day never ends at three o'clock. Many times after school, just for a mental break, I'll walk the halls. It's then that a sort of second shift begins for high school: sports practice, band practice, clubs, cheerleading, newspaper, yearbook—so much. Nearly every weekend there's a sporting event, and three times a year our theater kids put on a play."

She stopped talking for a moment, perhaps pleased to picture her world.

"And the crazy thing is, AJ, I love it. There's not one part of it I'd trade away." Glancing out the window and then at her stack of ungraded essays, she sighed gently. "Oh, fewer papers to grade wouldn't be the world's end." With a practiced motion, she pulled locks of hair and tucked them behind her ears. "So, coffee for me, although I'm really a tea woman, but I drained my stock two weeks ago and haven't found time to refill it." She tapped her forehead. "I'd better make a note of that or the tea will find the same fate as that nonexistent seat cushion. Hot chocolate for you?"

"Please."

She eased her chair from the desk, smiled, and strolled past me, her pretty eyes pinning me in place. "I won't be long."

With Miss Wells out of the room, I don't know what came over me, but I left my chair and went to hers. Because of casters attached to the chair's feet, it rolled easily across the wooden floor. Sitting in this direction, I had a better view of the bookshelves that were once behind me. Hardbound and softbound editions rested upright or flat with no evident stacking system. Unlike Mr. Billing's library, her books were not uniformly bound nor were they left unread, and some books wedged against one another or bulged with papers. The editions seemed better off that way, and I smiled to imagine a few of them actually finding a way to the ladder-back's seat.

Sitting in her chair where I didn't belong made me stretch all limits farther. I picked up the essay she had just graded, skimmed her marginalia, and then came to her note at the end.

James,

You have great ideas! You do a fine job of drawing differences among the characters' beliefs regarding success. Especially sharp is your choice to compare Gatsby and Nick. The essay, however, must be more convincing. To build an argument, you must provide ample evidence. When you cite examples from the text, you must include <u>more</u> *analysis. Explain* <u>why</u> *your support works. What helps your score is your vivid writing style! Apt words and phrases come naturally to you, and that is a rare talent!*

Keep working!

Because the note was personal, I wondered if James was a favorite student, so I sifted through the other graded essays and found that she had written a note to *every* student. I couldn't calculate how much extra time that had taken.

"AJ, grab this mug, but be…" Miss Wells entered and caught me sitting in her chair.

Embarrassed, I bolted upright. "Sorry, I was just seeing how…I was just seeing what… what things look like from this side of the desk." After fumbling over my words, I stumbled from the chair. I must have given her a love-struck, loopy look, an expression she probably recognized from many male students over the years, an expression she had caused to appear without ever trying.

"I see." She beamed. "Here, take this mug. But be careful; it's hot."

"Thanks." I sat on the stiff-seated chair and watched her organize student papers. Fading sunlight slanted through the solitary window and traced the profile of her face and hair with a winter-to-spring rosy hue. I wanted to sit across from her as long as possible.

"AJ, most teachers dread grading essays because it takes so long." With an enormous paperclip she clasped a class set. "It takes time, but it gives me a chance to communicate directly with each student. When people write, they want to communicate something to somebody." She grasped another group of papers and tapped them against the desk, making a neat stack. "So, I want every student to know I read *every* word. I write comments to turn the one-sided essay into a two-sided conversation."

"I bet they appreciate it."

"I hope so. Now," she pushed her piles of papers aside, "show me some flowers."

"Are you sure?"

"You're the only one I know selling flower seeds, so you have the market cornered. Besides, I need a new adventure."

I spread an assortment on her desk.

After studying the packs, she picked one up. "Pansies; that's for thoughts. If Ophelia mentioned it, I should choose it."

"A lot of people like that one, and it's a perennial."

"Right." She paused and I could tell an idea had come to her because her eyes widened. "You know something, that's *exactly* what I try to give my students."

"Flowers?"

She laughed. "No, not flowers, AJ." Her expression turned earnest. "Let's see. Do you like to read stories?"

"Yes."

"Why?"

"I like learning about people; what they do and what happens to them."

"That's right. And if the story is laudable, it will last. It doesn't matter if the people in the story are a different race or religion or nationality from you because all people share the same desires."

The way Miss Sarah Wells spoke—with conviction, excitement, and wonder—lifted me. Because she apparently believed her words, I believed them, too. I wanted always to believe them.

"As silly as it sounds, I see myself as an annual flower, someone who lives once, but literature—great literature—is perennial. It blooms forever. And that's what I try to give my students. Even if they remember just one line from a novel, a play, a story, or a poem, it's something they can keep throughout their lives."

Again, I remembered Mr. Billings and a dark thought crossed my mind. "Some people say that books and literature aren't practical."

She leaned toward me and whispered, "Neither are flowers." She smiled a dazzlingly smile. "If people see only practicality, they'll miss the beauty. There's a whole school of thought about that. You see, beauty doesn't need a reason."

"I wish people cared more about beauty than they do about money."

She nodded thoughtfully. "Money *is* necessary. But some people measure everything with a monetary yardstick. Does it seem right that society respects money, but it doesn't reward the people who add intangibles: knowledge or beauty? I don't know if that will ever change. But I do know, at a fairly young age, I've experienced what money can and cannot do. What it can and cannot hold. I think of my parents every day. Yes," she said solemnly, "I'm well aware of money's limits."

We sipped our drinks and after a few minutes any sign of somberness subsided until we sat easily, perhaps both of us lost in gentle thoughts. I felt the moment's tenderness and then wondered if Miss Wells longed for a man—a husband—to share the partner's desk.

"So, AJ, you're working toward a pocketknife?"

"Yes."

"You don't seem the pocketknife type. Oh, I know you're all boy, but I think you have a deeper layer to you." Her eyes fell heavily against me. "Are you sure it's a pocketknife you want?"

I clamped my lips, but my resolve weakened. "Well…"

"Tell me."

"I want a paint set. I'm working toward getting a starter's kit." I told her everything. About keeping the secret from my parents. I even told her Mrs. Billings was letting me paint in her studio.

"Mrs. Billings," she mused and then smiled a singular smile; the smile women use when talking about another woman without revealing their thoughts. "Yes, she's quite a gal."

"Do you know her?"

"Let's say I've heard more about her than I actually know about her." She looked at her coffee mug and then at the flower packets. "Don't worry. Your secrets are safe with me. Now, let's get you closer to that paint set." She pulled open the desk's center drawer, gathered four quarters, and chose columbines, pansies, violets, and zinnias.

"Thanks, Miss Wells." Then, although I knew I'd blush, I said it anyway: "I hope you're my English teacher next year."

"That would be nice, AJ, but I've received next year's schedule and it looks like I'll be teaching two junior level classes and three senior level ones.

"Oh."

"But don't worry. If you need help with English, you can visit my office or you can come here, even if you're not selling flowers."

"Thank you."

It was getting late but I didn't want to leave, and I saw she was right to have set her desk by this window because even with the fading sun, the room caught every bit of declining light; a spotlight lamp on top of her desk would soon brighten her workspace.

"Miss Wells, did you always want to be a teacher?"

"Since I was a girl."

"What do you like best about it?"

"AJ, you've told me a secret, so perhaps I owe you one." She looked at me in an unusual way, as if knowing I would understand. "Most people realize that a person who teaches English probably started her career by loving literature. That's true for me, but another love, a different love, came to me afterwards." Sarah Wells looked away and gazed past the window. "The classroom—my room—is more than a place filled with desks, books, and chairs. Sometimes, especially on cold winter days when the outside world is gray and grim, inside my classroom, when students fill every chair, and each girl and boy is writing an essay and pouring their hearts and minds into their words and our interior world is hushed, warm, and peaceful—it's then that I feel absolutely complete. I feel safe. And I know that moment is *life*."

For a full minute, her words lingered in the receding light and I would have given anything to stay with her, but she turned to me and said, "I'd ask you to supper, AJ, but I'm only heating a can of soup. Chicken noodle. Not an appetizing offer."

"It sounds fine to me."

"It does?" She laughed gently. "I'm glad because there are different nourishments. But I'm sure your mother wants you home where you can have something more substantial. As for me, a single gal, I often get by on soup and saltines." She smiled a roundabout smile. "Who knows? Maybe someday I'll whip up a family pot roast dinner?"

"I bet you'll make a great pot roast."

"Perhaps, perhaps." She looked toward her bookcases as the most delicate afternoon light glimmered on her cheek. "Oh, I deal with those 'evenings of the brain' now and then 'when not a moon disclose a sign or star come out within,' but I'm only twenty-eight years old. Still time." I didn't understand all she said, and then with a wave of her hand she brushed the words aside. "Come along, AJ. Time to make tracks."

By the front door, Miss Wells stood and placed her hands on her hips. "Honestly though, I don't know about that pot roast dinner. Another secret: the first time I made chicken noodle soup from a can, I forgot to add water." She laughed once more. "Even a sailor couldn't have swallowed that much salt."

***

We sat at the kitchen table. My father was in a good mood, the most upbeat I'd seen him in a long time, but my mother seemed more distant than ever. She'd been eating very little and that night was no exception. The macaroni and cheese she'd made didn't help. As always, it came from a box and a pouch; the cheese—a gooey, amber glob—could have plugged holes in Sheetrock.

"That's right. A three-week vacation this summer," my father repeated. "It took me years to get, but I earned it. And the overtime I've been working caught us up with all our payments. "

"That's great, Dad." I said and glanced at my mother who offered no reaction.

My father kept going. "I've never had that much time off, and you know what I'd like to do? I'd like to go camping a few days. What do you say, AJ?"

"Sure, I guess."

"Honey, what do you think? How does camping sound?"

Not lifting her eyes, she held a fork and mangled her food in a mindless way. "Camping sounds like camping."

I looked at my father who frowned but started in again.

"Maybe we could go fishing? Would you like that, AJ?"

"Sure." Actually, I would have enjoyed it. Even camping sounded good because we'd be in nature, and I loved the feel and smell of a forest.

"And I thought we could all go to a baseball game. To Yankee Stadium. AJ?"

"Sure, Dad, if it's not too much."

"We can do it. Maybe not box seats, but we'll be okay. Honey, what do you think?"

She dropped her fork onto the plate and knitted her fingers. "No baseball for me."

I knew she was on the verge of something terrible. Her limp hair hid most of her face, but her eyes wavered and her lips quivered.

My father scowled. Then he chose his words carefully. "I thought we all might take a road trip. You know, hop in the car and see a place we've never seen. Maybe up to Boston? Lots of historical things there. And just outside of Boston are plenty of small towns. Maybe we could stay at one of those old-time inns?"

I never heard my father talk this way. His words were cautious but his emotions were unrestrained as he painted a beautiful picture, and so, without qualifying anything, I said, "That would be great."

But I shouldn't have agreed with him because after I spoke my mother finally raised her head. The steel coil within her was about to snap. He should have seen this, too. He should have recognized the warning signs. Perhaps he did. But he didn't pull back.

"What do you say?" His voice was sharp now and aimed at my mother. "Where do you want to go?"

She looked at him with disbelief and then her lips widened into a hideous grin. All at once in a horrible way she shrieked and laughed together, a sound from deep inside her. Her shoulders shook. She tossed her head back and nearly choked on her cries. Senselessly, she grabbed her plate and slammed it against the table.

And then she left. I heard her footsteps along the uncarpeted hall, heard her open their bedroom door, heard it bang shut—and then I heard the lock click.

I bowed my head and waited. My father said nothing, didn't move. Then, like a bygone blacksmith, his fist pounded the table the way a hammer once pounded iron. He pushed his chair away, knocking it over, and then stalked after her.

I imagined what would happen next, picturing him rattling the doorknob and then breaking down the door, but somewhere in the hallway he stopped. Perhaps he second-guessed himself or he feared something. I don't know. But he turned back.

After walking past the kitchen table, he grabbed his keys from the counter, ripped open the side door, and lurched outside. I heard his truck start, and then I heard tires churning down the gravel.

I sat at the table for a long time and wondered if he had pushed her too hard, but I couldn't pinpoint what had caused my mother's reaction. But I knew something had fractured—a bond had broken. And I knew it was a breach that could never be bridged.

***

The next day I hurried home after school and found my mother in the living room. She had my father's club chair turned toward the window and sat so still, I thought she may have stopped breathing.

"Kevin invited me over for dinner," I told her and practically ran to my room to pick up my zippered pouch and box of seeds. Then I raced to the kitchen, grabbed an apple from a big plastic bowl sitting on the counter, and stuffed it inside the box. "I'll try to sell packets before I go to Kevin's." I stood on the edge of the family room at least six feet from her.

"I don't think," she said flatly, "your father will be home tonight."

It was unnerving to see her sitting so lifelessly. With or without him in the house, I didn't want to be there.

"I'll be home later."

"Your father…" she said, but I headed for the door. "Your goddamned father…"

I left the house, glad not to hear another word.

Earlier that day I had decided to call on the Smith sisters. They lived on the farthest edge of the neighborhood and between my house and theirs was Moccasin Pond, so it made the perfect stopping place. I could be alone.

After reaching the pond, I found a familiar spot. Decades ago a white oak tree divided into twins, and at some point lightning hit one tree, severing it. For as long as I knew, that massive part of the tree was a log, and sitting on it, a person could rest his back against the tree remaining upright. Now, in early April, Moccasin Pond lay in an unsettled state. From the pond's center and to its fringes, ice formed an island. But from its fringes to its edges, in a jagged circumference, water lapped the land. So, at this stage, what was this body of nature? Not safe for skating; not fit for water fowls; not completely liquid or solid. It maintained an odd existence. It was a unique, fixed place, perhaps having no defined purpose or perhaps having a purpose undefined.

I sat on the worn log and ate my apple, thinking it would be my dinner because Kevin had not invited me over. Sitting there within the forest's stillness and its undertone of stirring life, I realized I would never marry. I was meant to be alone. Not a hermit, exactly, but a solitary being, not unlike the indefinite body of water that lay before me. No river, ocean, or tributary touched it. The pond was self-contained. Likewise and deliberately, at that moment I knew my interactions with the outward world would be limited, and I would maintain a fixed, inward place. But at that time I didn't know the price I'd pay.

Being in their mid-seventies, the Smith sisters didn't work, so I knew they'd be home. They lived in a ranch house, one of the oldest in the neighborhood, painted a forest green. The place stood far back from the street and a half dozen gigantic evergreens had overgrown the grounds. The house blended so well with the pines, it was almost invisible. Walking toward it, I thought of an enchanted cottage, and later in life, with a dose of imagination, I transformed the Smith sisters' house into a setting for some of my stories.

After knocking on the front door with its peeling varnish and splintered wood, I heard a padding of steps. When the door opened, one sister, Miss Myra—a petite, lissome woman—stood quietly with anticipation. Her brown eyes squinted, widened, and squinted again.

"Hi, Miss Smith. I live across the way. And I…"

"Oh, gracious, I know who you are, AJ. Come in." A look of delight filled her. "Come in and tell me what brings you to our neck of the woods."

I stepped inside and smelled something delightful cooking. Holding the cardboard box to my chest, I said, "I'm selling packets of flower seeds, and I'm wondering if you'd like to buy some."

A smile lit the old woman's face that hardly held a wrinkle. "Is that so? Well, come to the kitchen." She turned, steadied herself, and walked carefully with an erect carriage. Her honey-colored housedress with a white ruffle had buttons from her chest to her shins. "Jenny and I," she said in a delicate voice, "would love to see what you're selling."

"No, Jenny would *not* like to see what you're selling." A gravelly voice sounded from another room. "And we don't need a fool salesman barging into this house with…. Oh."

As we stepped into the kitchen, the sister sitting at the long rectangular table saw me. Miss Myra said, "Jenny, we have a guest."

"I can see that now."

"And he's selling packets of flower seeds."

"How do you like that? A guest and salesman rolled into one," she huffed.

While both women had gray tresses, their physical similarities stopped there. Myra Smith was dainty with a slim figure, and her manners and movements were as modest as her clothing. Jenny Smith, on the other hand, was a barrel-shaped woman with a square, rugged face that looked as weathered as the house's front door. She wore a red flannel shirt beneath denim overalls that looked as though they'd seen a thousand acres of work. Her sturdy hand, like a bear's paw, engulfed a pencil as she wrote numbers into a ledger. The women didn't look like sisters at all.

"I'm sure Jenny won't mind looking at the flowers," Miss Myra said to me. "I'll finish adding spices to the beef stew." She pointed toward four tiny glass jars on the counter and a boiling pot on the stove. Like the Novellos' meal, the aroma made my stomach rumble.

I looked cautiously at Miss Jenny who apparently had taken my measure. "I've learned," she said, "that a pint-sized salesman always tries to sell a gallon of goods. But just hold on a minute, young fella." She licked the pencil's tip and added a notation to her ledger. Her nose was wide and her lips thin, reminding me of George Washington's picture on the dollar bill. "I'm just figuring the monthly expenses." Soon, she pushed the small book aside. "So, what have you got there?"

I had repeated the action of displaying the seeds many times, and my stock was thin, but the colorful packets still looked attractive, especially against the white painted but soiled kitchen table. Miss Jenny leaned forward and separated the packs. Clearly, she was a take-charge, no-nonsense person.

"Hollyhocks," she said with interest. "We had those on the farm. Ma planted them along the walkway to our house. As a girl I remember measuring my height against them when they grew tall in summer." Even when recounting a sentimental memory, her voice remained gruff.

"I can see your doing that," her sister said and added a tablespoon of spice into the steaming stockpot. After placing a lid over the pot, she joined us at the table.

"So, how much are the packets?" Miss Jenny asked.

"Twenty-five cents."

"Used to be ten cents."

"Don't be such a skinflint," Miss Myra said with a laugh.

"Upbringing, I suppose." She looked at me. "Say, do you have any Indian Pipes?"

I didn't have Indian Pipes; in fact, I'd never heard of them. "No, ma'am."

"Too bad."

"I'm sure we can find other flowers," her sister consoled. "Why did you want those?"

"Just foolishness."

"You're many things, Sister, but foolish is not one of them."

"Well," the woman straightened her shoulders and hitched the straps of her overalls, "a sketch of Indian Pipes was on the first book of Emily Dickinson's poems, and because I'm going to use a line from one of her poems for my book title, I thought of growing that flower."

The image of this roughhewn woman as a writer jarred me, so, unable to keep my surprise in check, I blurted out: "You're writing a book?"

"Do you think a woman can't write a book?" she asked indignantly. "Or do you think a woman like *me* can't write a book?"

"Dear, take off the boxing gloves. He's only a boy."

"Heck, it's never too soon to step out of the cave."

The sisters glanced at each other and shared a knowing look. With a kind voice, Miss Myra said, "My sister has lived a remarkable life, and she's writing about it."

Miss Jenny raised her chin. "They call it a memoir."

After my embarrassment passed, my interest grew. "What's it about?"

Miss Myra's small hands braced against the table and pushed herself from it. "Why don't you tell him about it, Jenny? I'll fire the kettle and make tea."

"Do you really want to hear it, boy?"

"Yes, I do."

"All right. Here's the *Reader's Digest* version." The imposing woman spoke like a natural story-teller. "I grew up on a farm about a hundred miles from here. A hundred miles is far, but it's only distance. Well sir, memory shortcuts distance. Now that I'm a relic, I've been thinking backwards." From her overalls' pocket she pulled a pack of Winston's and had a cigarette between her lips and lit faster than any man could do it. "We had forty-two acres, and Pa expected me to do the same work as my brother Bill, who was three years older, so I learned to mend fences, plow and plant, how to bring in a harvest, and how to drive and fix a tractor. It was a hard life, but I didn't know no better. For me, it was just the way of things. And in most ways it was good. Yes sir, I felt good about working the land and making things grow. And Ma took care of everything else. Quite a woman. Naturally strong and smart. Always with a smile and a prayer. A lot like Myra she was. Then, the day after I turned thirteen, Pa died. Threshing accident. Never understood it because he had common sense and was sure-handed." Her eyes squinted as she drew hard on the cigarette.

"Anyway, for the next five years, me and Bill worked the farm while Ma faded a little more each day. Then she died. Never knew what killed her, but after Pa went, I guess you could say she died too. Oh, she went on living but it wasn't a real life. She sort of became a ghost; saying hardly a word; not doing hardly a thing. It was a dark time. Me and Bill had her buried next to Pa.

"By that time Bill had put himself through the community college. Hell, I dropped out of school when I was sixteen. Anyhow, the two of us couldn't keep up the farm, and Bill said if we sold it, his share could pay for real college classes and get him an accounting degree. Besides, he'd had his fill of farm work. Funny thing was, I didn't mind it."

With a skilled hand and two trips, Miss Myra set three cups, saucers, a sugar bowl, a creamer, and a china teapot on the table. Then she poured hot tea into each cup. "I expect you like your tea sweet, as I do," she said.

"Yes, if that's all right."

"Of course. Two teaspoons?"

"Please."

Miss Jenny picked up her story, seemingly absorbed in it. "So, we sold the farm. I was eighteen, restless, and knew something inside me didn't fit right, so I took my share of the cash and headed west. Went all over. Colorado, Wyoming, Montana, Idaho. Some pretty country; some barren places, too. Had me some good times and a bunch of bad times. Worked at truck stops, ranches, on highway crews, and gimme-another-shot-of-whiskey bars. But telling you about all them adventures would be the long version. I've recorded them days in my book."

"*Those* days," Miss Myra corrected.

"Right." Miss Jenny came to the end of her cigarette and crushed the filter into an ashtray. "But I grew up in the East and something always pulled me to go back. So, after seven years of drifting across mountains and plains, I hitchhiked home." Without looking, she snapped a stick match with her thumb and lit another cigarette. Somehow I didn't mind the smell of her cigarette smoke the way I did my mother's. "Once I got back, I knocked around for a few years. Sometimes working two jobs at a time: gas stations, 7-Elevens, and delivering newspapers. But then I saw a Help Wanted sign in Flynn's Hardware window.

She snorted a laugh. "Old Sean Flynn was so damned stiff and proper, he didn't want to hire a woman, but I made him walk the store with me." She smiled proudly. "Well sir, I pointed out a bunch of things like the different grits of sandpaper and their uses, and the difference between a female adaptor from a male adaptor in plumbing connections, and how to wire a three-way switch, and why one paintbrush works best with an oil-based paint, and why galvanized nails are the ones you need for fence pickets. Stuff like that. After I showed old Flynn I knew more about hardware than he did, he give me the job. I worked there forty-three years. You could say I did my share. So, enough was enough."

"My father goes to Flynn's Hardware all the time."

"Yeah. I remember your father. Hard worker, though a little strange in his ways." She squeezed another lungful of smoke from her cigarette. "So, Flynn's son took over the business about fifteen years ago. College degree and all, but not half the brains his father had, neither was he half the man. And I don't see a small place like that lasting much longer when they're building those big-ass stores out along the highway. Yes sir, soon enough them big dogs will gobble up all of them little pups."

I thought of Flynn's Hardware store in our town center along with the bank, bakery, grocer, beauty salon, barber shop, diner, and drug store with a soda fountain, and how they all suddenly seemed vulnerable.

Miss Myra returned to the stove and removed the lid from the round pot. She dipped a wooden spoon into the stew and tasted the broth. "Might need more salt."

"For the love of cow pies," her sister said with exasperation, "you would add salt to a salt lick."

Miss Myra curled her left hand into a tiny fist and placed it on her hip. "What do *you* know about cooking?"

"Nothing, except what tastes good and what don't."

"You mean 'what *doesn't*.'"

"In my memoir you can correct my words and commas and such, but *not* when I'm talking."

"I see. And I see we need an impartial judge around here." She dipped the spoon into the pot. "AJ, you are the chosen one." Standing by my side and lowering the spoon to my lips, a savory smell tickled my nose. Then I swallowed the broth.

"Wow," I said. "I wouldn't add more salt. It's perfect."

"There," said Miss Jenny, "I knew it."

"Oh, I knew it was perfect all along," her sister said with a twinkle in her eyes. "Just needed verification. Well, I'll let that simmer awhile." She rejoined us at the table.

We drank tea and sat in a calm silence, unlike the silence shrouding my family's meals. But a question had been bobbing inside me, and I didn't know the right way to ask it. Maybe there wasn't a right way. I turned toward Miss Myra. "Miss Smith, did you grow up on the same farm as your sister?"

The two women looked at each other, then at their teacups, and then at each other again. Perhaps thoughts passed between them. Then Miss Jenny's chin nodded once as if granting permission.

"No," Miss Myra said. "I grew up not far from here. A middle-class home in a middle-class town. Unlike Jenny, I've never traveled anywhere." She sighed. "I suppose that's why I bought that Hummel years ago. It's called the Merry Wanderer." She pointed toward a small, colorful figurine standing on the windowsill, a young lad with a spring in his step, clutching an umbrella in one hand and a carpetbag in the other. "No," she said, "my adventures all happened in the books I've read."

Miss Jenny tapped out another cigarette from her Winston pack. "It's a good thing Myra has read so many books. She gave me the title for my memoir: *Accustomed to the Dark*."

"But," I stammered and then let it out: "you both have the same last name."

Miss Myra lowered her eyes. "Smith is a common name."

"You're not sisters?"

"No. No, my life has been quite different from Jenny's. In high school I took many business and secretarial classes. I loved literature but the only thing to do with that background was to be a teacher; however, my parents didn't have the money to send a girl to college. So, after I graduated high school I found a job a few towns over. Here in Kenton. I worked at the Kenton Savings and Loan."

"Mr. Billings' bank?"

"Yes, but he wasn't there when I began my employment. Luckily though, after he arrived and eventually became the bank president, he kept me on."

"He'd be a one-legged stool to let you go."

Miss Myra sipped her tea and said, "Your opinion might be a tad biased."

"Biased my butt. Hell, you're a damned good worker, and you're smarter than that arrogant halfwit will ever be. I knew you was smart the minute we met."

"Where did you meet?"

Miss Myra looked at me with an expression that said, I might as well tell it all. "We met at the Vesta Diner."

Faster than quicksilver, Miss Jenny lit a third cigarette and then rested her elbows on the table, looking anxious, as if she'd waited a long time to tell someone this chapter. "I worked at Flynn's Hardware and Myra worked at the bank. We'd seen each other before but had never met, let alone had a conversation. One day I took my usual late lunch at two o'clock."

"And I took an unusual late lunch. You see, I always ate lunch at noon, but this day the bank had pressing business that had to be concluded before the close of day, so we all pushed on through the lunch hour."

"The diner was near empty, but for some reason, yes sir, we both chose to sit at the counter. You know them round stools?"

"The ones that spin in a circle?"

"Yeah. So, we sat with two seats between us."

"And we ordered the same meal: tuna salad sandwich on rye bread with cole slaw."

"And iced tea."

"And iced tea," Miss Myra echoed with pleasure. "So, we started talking."

"Yes sir, we got to talking and one thing led to another." The two women locked eyes. "After I'd given out hope, I found what was missing inside me."

"And I found the same missing piece."

We were all silent again, and I tried to understand everything they had told me, but I was too young then.

"So, we continued. After awhile, and because we have the same last name, we told people we were sisters. It wasn't hard because no one had really noticed either of us before. Yes, we did things sisters or friends would do like shopping or eating at restaurants or going to movies."

"I guess people didn't think much about it." Miss Jenny puffed her cigarette. "We never bothered nobody; we were never much of any consequence."

"To make our lives easier, we bought this house about twenty years ago."

"At that time hardly a soul lived out here."

"Just a handful of people with distance between them. Now, so many new homes have gone up!"

"I liked it better before. Too damned crowded now."

"Yes, distance let us 'step to a different drummer however measured or far away.'"

"Isn't she something?" Miss Jenny asked with pride. "She's always quoting somebody. I know that, but I never know *who* she's quoting."

Miss Myra patted her 'sister's' hand. "It doesn't matter."

Reaching across the table, Miss Jenny grasped a black-and-white, marbled composition book. "Well, without you this thing would never be written."

"Is that your memoir?"

"Part of it. I got three other books just like it—all filled." Against the ashtray she snubbed out her cigarette before it was finished. "Myra thinks we might get it published, but I'm not sure."

"It's quite a story, and it has something to say to people who feel lost, to people who feel as if they don't fit anywhere. In time, I hope certain things will change."

"I doubt it." Miss Jenny leaned back in her chair. "Years ago when I was in Wyoming, an old rancher told me something I'll never forget. He said, 'There are two great American myths. One, today is not as good as yesterday, and two, tomorrow will be better than today.'"

Miss Myra rose from the table and cleared cups and saucers. "I'm not sure everything works that way, Sister. Someday folks will realize that people have more similarities than differences." She placed the chinaware into the sink and returned for the sugar bowl and creamer. "Everyone needs to be needed, and everyone needs love."

I stood up to help her, but she shooed me back in place.

"Maybe that part is true, and that's what bothers me because today, instead of distance, we have isolation. There's a difference between the two. It seems the more we move forward, the more isolated we become."

Over her shoulder Miss Myra said in a simple way, "Yes, isolation leads to fear, and fear leads to hatred." She wiped her hands on a dishtowel. "But keep working on your book, Sister, because you never know what good will come of it. It just may help someone bridge that gap of isolation."

"We'll see."

As she opened the notebook and thumbed through its pages, a question came to me. "You said the title is from a poem?"

"That's right. Of course, without Myra I never would have known it."

"What's the poem about?"

"Well, it talks about dealing with things that happen to you. Rotten things. Yes sir, things you don't expect or deserve."

From the stockpot, Miss Myra lifted its lid and steam enveloped her like a luminous cloud. "Yes, that's true," she said, "but it's also about adjusting to hardships and enduring dark times."

Although the room was warm and light, shadows started their late afternoon march, so Miss Myra switched on the overhead light. Because I'd eaten nothing since lunch except for the apple at Moccasin Pond, I was hungry. When the 'sisters' asked me to stay for dinner, I was glad to accept. The beef stew was fantastic, and Miss Myra's biscuits were better than any I've eaten since. She attributed their flakiness and flavor to buttermilk and "a few secret sprites." Our conversation was minimal, but our lack of words produced security, not tension. Best of all, the easy, intimate way the women ate and savored the meal rendered time unhurried.

After supper Miss Jenny said we ought to get down to business. Without hesitation she picked eight seed packets—the largest sale I ever made—and paid me with two well-traveled dollar bills.

"What's your commission?" she asked.

I didn't know what she meant, so Miss Myra said, "How much of the sales money do you keep?"

I explained the selling and redemption process.

"What do you figure on getting?"

"A pocketknife."

"Smart choice. If that's what you want." She turned to her journal, and I thanked them for the sale and the food. As I gathered my things, Miss Myra offered to walk me to the door, but Miss Jenny stopped us. "AJ, in this household we have division of labor. Myra tends to the inside and I tend to the outside, and you might have noticed I'm no longer a spring chicken, so when them flower seeds get here, it'd be a good turn if you'd help me with the planting. Will you do that?"

"Yes, ma'am, I'd like to."

"All right," she said, tapped out another cigarette, and opened her journal.

A moment later, standing by the front door, Miss Myra's right hand grasped the handle as her left hand clutched my elbow. She looked at me the way a benign teacher would look at a young student. "We talked about many things this afternoon, AJ."

"Yes, ma'am."

"And words, my young friend, are powerful, and their meanings can shift. Depending on semantics, the word 'sister' has many meanings. The way I see it, there's no point in telling people something they don't need to know. It's better that way." Her tender eyes found mine as her forceful hand gripped my arm, and I realized then what Mr. Carter had meant when he described this woman as being gentle but strong. "Otherwise, people question things that are different, and then they create answers. And some answers are cold, cramped, and dark as a grave. Do you understand?"

"No, ma'am. But I won't say anything about you two not being sisters if that's what you mean. Promise."

She nodded and released my arm. "Stop by in late May and give Jenny a hand planting those flowers. With your help, they should grow just fine."

She switched on the porch light because clouds had rolled in and made the dim skies dark. I had not reached the street when she turned off the light, most likely not knowing I still needed it. I stopped walking, unable to see for the sudden darkness. Then, either the clouds passed or my eyes adjusted to the lack of light. I stepped forward, hesitated, and stepped again.

EIGHT

A few days after my visit with the Smith sisters and for my final stop, I chose Judge Franklin's place. As long as anyone could remember, Judge Monroe Franklin lived in the large house perched on a hill. His place sat on a truncated road, and because the Judge had purchased the adjoining acreage years ago, the house stood alone. Nearly engulfing the place was an unspoiled forest full of hardwoods and pines.

Monroe Franklin had been a successful lawyer and for the final eleven years of his professional career, he served as a judge. So, people referred to him as Judge Franklin. As a younger man—you can tell from the old photographs that sometime appear in the local paper— he was a robust, handsome figure, and even now, after having lost weight and muscle, he still looked manly. He had always been aloof, but my father told me that after his wife died, the Judge turned everyone and everything completely aside.

It was mid-afternoon and I faced a long, steep climb to the house, and because the driveway was dirt and stones, it was hard to ascend without slipping every second or third step. My father had also told me that people believed the Judge kept it that way to discourage visitors. Why did I bother with Judge Franklin? We had never met, and he had a reputation for being cranky. But after stopping at so many houses and visiting so many people, I felt bolder than when I had first started. And somehow, selling seed packets or earning a prize or even being resourceful didn't matter. Because this solitary, old man remained a mystery, my curiosity outstripped my caution. I had to see him for myself.

The Federal-style house kept its original lines: no additions, no extensions, and no portico above the front steps. The clapboard was white, the shutters navy, and the front door red; however, the accumulated seasons had taken their toll, so colors faded and siding flaked. It was sad to see the house neglected.

I trekked up the driveway to where a flagstone path led to the front door. I paused and asked myself if I really wanted to ring the doorbell when a sudden, unfamiliar noise startled me. It was a high-pitched, whirring sound that rose to a higher pitch, dropped down for a few seconds, and then stopped. The noise came from an outbuilding and I saw two tire ruts leading to a wooden structure—a large shed that probably once served as a single-car, detached garage. The outbuilding's unpainted boards had grayed, and tree limbs—budding with spring's arrival—stretched over the roof from both sides. An enormous gate-like door hung wide open, and as I approached, I found that the shed's interior was now a workshop; the sound I'd heard came from a table saw. Standing by the saw with his back to me and holding a piece of wood was a man wearing a denim shirt and ragged jeans.

"Judge Franklin?"

He looked up and turned toward me slowly. Facing me, he reminded me of that recruitment poster of Uncle Sam wearing a top hat and pointing his finger at you, only the Judge was without a hat, a mustache, or a beard.

"AJ, is it?"

"Yes, sir. I didn't think you knew me."

"I don't." He turned away and ambled toward the workbench. "What do you want?"

I moved closer. "I'm selling flower seeds, and I'm wondering if you'd like to buy some."

The Judge squared the piece of wood he'd just cut against another piece. They looked identical. "Young fella," he said while squinting at the boards' lengths, "I like your straight-forward approach, but do you see any flowers on this property?"

"No, sir."

"Uh, huh. That should answer your question." He set the boards on the workbench.

I stepped inside the shed. Three naked lightbulbs, three feet from each other, hung from the roof's main crossbeam. The dust-coated bulbs offered little light, but sunshine snuck through the shed's chinks and knotholes, and along with the open gate-door, the place was shadowy but not dark. A blended, not unpleasant smell of lumber, grass clippings, gasoline, motor oil, treadless tires, tools, rodent traces, loam, and insect sprays pervaded the place. The workbench had a wood vise at one end and a bunch of hand tools scattered on its stained and scarred surface. I stepped close to the Judge as he gazed through the lone window that lightened the workbench.

"What are you building?"

"Right now this project doesn't look like much, but it's taking shape. Here, feel this piece." The board shook a bit in his quivering hand.

I held the piece, four inches wide and three feet long. It was solid and its surface was smooth. "I like how it feels. What kind of wood is it?"

"Ash."

"Don't they make baseball bats from ash?"

"That's right." He gave a surprised look. "Very impressive."

"So, what are you building?"

"A cradle for a grandchild."

"Very impressive." We both smiled.

"Well then, you're selling flower seeds?"

"Yes, sir."

"Why?"

I told him about the pocketknife and how close I was to earning it.

He gave a short grunt. "AJ, possessions grow obsolete, or we outgrow them. *Experience* is what you want." He placed the board back on the bench and rubbed his chin. Gray, spare stubble showed several days' growth. "Experiences live within us, young fella. They make us who we are."

A slideshow of faces flickered within me: the families I've described and the families I met but haven't mentioned.

"Tell you what, young man." He pointed to the rafters. "See those folding chairs hanging from those hooks?"

"Yes."

"Get that ladder over there, climb up, and bring down two chairs. Set them outside where we can feel the sun."

The five-foot wooden ladder was heavy and creaked when I mounted it. After two climbs, I had both chairs down.

"I've been on my feet too long," he said and sank into one of the vinyl chairs. "Come on, Son, sit down." I did and felt at once that the chair had seen better days, but the early spring air was pleasant as it nudged and teased nature to transform the world from grays to greens. "Yes," he continued, "I used to care a great deal about possessions. I should have cared about significant matters." He looked off and was silent for a long moment. Then he spoke in a low, barely audible voice. "My wife always wanted to see Europe. She used to cut out features from newspapers and collected brochures from travel agencies. Oh, we took vacations—practical trips here and there—but I told her to wait until I retired and we'd take the grand tour. Laura and I were the same age, so I targeted my retirement at sixty-five, and that's when I retired. Laura died at sixty-three. That was eight years ago." Trembling fingers brushed against his faltering lips. "I should have given her more experiences, not *things*."

The Judge's pale blue eyes grew moist, staring into some private place. He gripped the chair but his arms twitched.

"Possessions. Yes, young man," he scowled, "For years I drove Cadillacs. Parked them right there." He pointed toward the shed. "Covered the car every night with a special tarp. Ha. All the time, money, and effort I spent on rubbish."

I looked over my shoulder. "You don't have a car now?"

"I don't need one."

"Not even to go to the A&P?"

"No. I have canned foods and vegetables right here and plenty of store-bought soups. I'm set for months. Besides, I don't eat much anymore. Now let me tell you something, young fella," he pointed a bony finger at me, "don't eat anything wrapped in plastic. Plastic is poison. Heck, the way things are going, someday *everything* will be wrapped in plastic." He nodded emphatically. "And go easy on meat and dairy products."

"Why?"

"Different reasons. Actually, when I think about it," he said with a quick laugh, "I once believed a good diet guaranteed good health. So much for that belief." He shifted his weight and apparently his thoughts shifted too. "About five years ago a close friend of mine died. I visited him before his passing and he said to me, 'I will leave this world a better place than I found it.' I got to thinking about that and decided it's impossible to leave the world that way. From cradle to grave we take, we clutter, we consume. Simply by existing, we deplete. For decades I used to compost, but I gave that up. You see, no matter how hard we try to do the right thing, we only make things worse." He spoke without anger or bitterness, with no emotion at all. He licked his lips and looked at me. "Not used to talking so much. I could use a glass of lemonade. Are you thirsty, AJ?"

"Sure."

"Good. Tell you what, go inside that door," he pointed to the house's side door. "It leads straight to the kitchen. In the refrigerator is a pitcher of lemonade I made this morning. Find some glasses, fill them, and bring them out here. Got that?"

"Yes, sir."

Walking into that kitchen was like walking back in time. The refrigerator, stove, and sink were old, small, and white. The cabinets were painted white and fastened to frames with black, wrought-iron hardware. The floor looked like a checkerboard of white and black square tiles. After opening the refrigerator with its antiquated pull handle, I grabbed the pitcher of lemonade and set it on the counter. I opened the cabinet nearest the sink and, sure enough, found glasses.

Outside, I handed the Judge his lemonade. Grasping the drink, his arm shook badly so that more than a few drops sputtered to the grass. To lessen the shaking, he gripped the glass with both hands.

"On top of everything else," he said. "I have palsy. Yes, 'a few, sad, last, gray hairs.'" He sighed. "You see, in college I majored in history but minored in English." He drank the lemonade with staggered gulps. "We're far from summer, but I knew it would be warm today, so I made lemonade this morning. How do you like it?"

"It's really good."

"Not too sweet?"

"No."

"It's easy to make, but people go for the ready-made stuff. I wonder if people know what they want or if they just follow what other people want? Take that pocketknife of yours. Not much call for a pocketknife these days, especially in suburbia. Is that what you want, or did someone suggest it? Like your father?" He nodded tellingly. "I know your father. And your mother. Probably better than you do. Heck, I know just about everyone in town. It's not hard to keep tabs on things in a small town, even from a distance." He looked at me, perhaps trying to read my thoughts.

I swallowed hard. "No, sir, it was my idea."

"Uh huh." He stared off again, turning his pallid face toward the sun. "Let me tell you a story. When I was a young man, nineteen years old, I finished my freshman year of college, and through a family connection on my mother's side, I had an opportunity to spend a summer out West. I worked as a volunteer for the National Park

Service in Montana. Extraordinary country. Have you been out West?"

"No, sir."

"Maybe someday you will. On seeing that wild, open country, my first thought was if a person wanted to get away from everything, this was the place." The Judge moved his chair so that the yellow sunlight soaked his face and shoulders. "So, after working in that majestic land for months, I developed a love for it and a conviction that forestry was my calling. I truly believed I was meant to live a spartan life within nature. I imagined living on the barest essentials and limiting my interactions with people." He glanced around. "I suppose that's why I've let things grow wild here now. It wasn't always that way because the civilized world had snared me." He coughed and then he couldn't stop coughing. It went on for a full minute until he wheezed and retched and spit out globs of bloody phlegm. After another minute, he breathed normally again, wiped sweat from his face, and recovered himself.

"Sorry, young fella. One of the auxiliary benefits."

I wasn't sure what he meant, but I managed to say, "That's all right."

"Let's see now. Oh yes. Yes, for many years I was intent on having a manicured property—the best-looking place around. Lord, how much time and worry I wasted on such foolishness! How far from myself had I traveled!"

"Why didn't you stay out West?

"That, AJ, is the sixty-four dollar question. Oh, I formulated a thoughtful scheme. I realized if I stayed with forestry, I would earn a paltry income. Therefore, my plan included supplementing my salary by building things: small, simple pieces of furniture, which I would sell. You see, I was always good with my hands." His serene expression turned sour. "But when I presented the idea to my father, he reacted as though the world had spun off its axis. The man was a lawyer, and by God his son would be a lawyer." The Judge drank more lemonade and then cleared his throat. "He gave me a choice: return to college where he'd pay all expenses or return to the West and he'd disown me."

"Geez, that's not much of a choice."

"It certainly was not. And it set me on a course I never really wanted. I spent years blaming him for derailing my dreams; however, later I realized it was my fault. I simply lacked the courage to defy him. I was young and untested. So, I followed a well-traveled path.

"Throughout law school I told myself that if I must be a lawyer, I'd be the type to defend people with limited means, but I soon learned that was difficult. And naturally it paid poorly." He ran a wavering hand through his gray hair. "While my contemporaries were moving up in the world—making the grade—I was flunking. It's human nature to compare yourself to those around you, especially those in the same profession who obtain positions and wealth in leaps and bounds. To make matters worse, some of my dire clients were so damned greedy. They wanted more than justice.

They wanted a lot of money for the most unrighteous cases. Hell, they were greedier than the lawyers. And that's saying something.

"And so, young fella, as the years passed, I rejected who I wanted to be and became consumed with the world's trappings." He looked at me with resignation. "I became my father."

My thoughts careened and without caution I said, "It was my father's idea about the pocketknife." I took a deep breath. "I want a paint set, a starter set."

"You like to paint?"

"Yes, and I might be good at it. And when I paint, I lose myself." I hesitated but pushed ahead. "I forget everything. The noise, the anger, the confusion. Do you know what I mean?"

"No. But I've read about people like that. Artists. And their work speaks for them. And the great artist produces work that exceeds himself. It speaks to everyone." After a pause, he said, "What will your art say?"

"I don't know."

"Fair enough. You have time to decide."

He rubbed his chin. "My job was restricted. I judged people through a fixed grid called 'the law.' That was easy. What would be hard? To judge people through an unfixed grid called 'the soul.'"

We were quiet for awhile, and then the man steadied himself to place his drink on the ground. After, he sat upright and rubbed his hands gingerly. "How would you like to help with that cradle?"

The question surprised but excited me. "Can I?"

"Absolutely."

In the shed I watched as he clamped one of the cut boards onto the workbench. Then he plugged in a compact, handheld machine. "This is a finishing sander," he said and lifted it so I could see a piece of sandpaper attached to its underside. "Just run this up and down over the wood. We want it as smooth as the piece you held. Here." He handed me the sander. It was a Sears Craftsman model with heft. "This is the power switch." He pointed to the on/off button built into the handle. "Are you ready?"

"Yes, sir."

"All right. Move it up and down *with* the grain, and don't press too hard. Let the sander do the work."

I flicked the switch and the small machine's strong vibration caught me off-guard, but I held on and moved the sander correctly. A layer of fine dust bubbled along the board. After five minutes of sanding, the Judge tapped my shoulder.

"Let's take a look." He brushed away the sawdust and felt the board. "Say now, *that* is quality work." I touched the wood, pleased that it felt just like the one he had sanded.

"Are there other boards to sand?"

"Two more if you want."

"Sure."

"All right. You can sand; I need to cut."

His table saw was set to rip a wide piece of wood into a narrow piece. He ran a board along the machine's fence, so close to the blade that he used a guide to push the wood through. The machine skirled like before, and I was glad not to be the one having his fingers near a spinning, slicing blade, especially fingers that shook so badly. So, I sanded the boards, and after fifteen minutes the Judge shut off the table saw.

"That's all for now," he said, a bit out of breath. "I can't stay on my feet too long." He tightened his belt a notch. "Let's sit outside."

We sat and drank more lemonade. The spring day was the kind that made you feel optimistic because you knew—or thought you knew—winter had finally passed. And yet nature's imminent tasks were arduous: trees must force leaves to open, birds must root for nesting stock, and flowers must crack through compacted earth.

After awhile, I thought to say: "I bet that cradle will be perfect when you're finished."

He laughed gently. "Nothing manmade is perfect, AJ. But that's all right." Carefully, he grasped his glass of lemonade and brought it to his lips. He drank and seemed to savor the sweet-sour taste. "You see, that cradle will be flawed, just like humanity is flawed. But it will hold the best of humanity, which is love. I understood that once, but I forgot it along the way."

"You mean, when you were a lawyer?"

"Yes. And I was worse as a judge." He looked off again, as though it were easier to talk to the wilderness. With the passing day, the sun had moved on, leaving him mostly in shadow but a crescent of light illuminated his profile, making his lips appear awfully thin and his nose seemed curved like an eagle's. "That's exactly what I did: I judged everyone. Maybe because, deep down, I was disappointed in myself—the person I had become. I stopped looking for the good in people. And now, it's too late." He turned to me with watery, blue eyes. "You see, I have a terminal cancer. The doctors told me, at best, I have four months to live." He smiled weakly. "You're the only person I've told."

"I…I'm sorry."

"Yes, at seventy-one years old, I was hoping for a better season. But that was an unwise hope. After all those years as a lawyer and a judge, I should know that justice is only a concept." He sipped more of his drink. "But do you know what my biggest regret is?"

"No, sir."

"It's not tied to places or wealth or possessions. No, I regret not being kinder to people. You see, so little changes from one year to the next, and our species shows no real progress. Not only do generations repeat mistakes, each generation creates new ones. We determinedly march to darkness. But kindness staves off darkness. Kindness is light. Being kinder to people wouldn't have taken much effort. And I should have started with my only child, my son."

His chin slumped onto his chest. For a moment I thought his heart had failed; panic dashed through me. I tensed but then moved toward him. Before reaching him, he raised his head, looked exhausted, but then held up both hands to signal he was all right. "Just give me a minute."

When he regained some color and breathed normally again, I wanted to offer some comfort. "Judge Franklin, you're building a cradle, and your son will appreciate that. One day your grandchild will, too."

He looked awfully tired. "AJ, my son and I are not on good terms. The last time I saw him, he was here for his mother's funeral. Our time together didn't go well." He frowned. "I barely know his wife, and they have no children. I don't know if they ever will."

"Then, why are you building a cradle?"

"Ha. Another good question, young man. We can chalk up my endeavor to something I finally learned— or relearned. You see, we must have faith in the future. 'Do I contradict myself? Very well, then I contradict myself.' Ha! Yes, we must look to the future—with all its wonders, uncertainties, and horrors." He crossed his arms against his chest. "AJ, I'm going to close my eyes for awhile. Don't worry; I'm fine. But I'd appreciate it if you'd stay here until I've rested."

In fact, we both closed our eyes. It was better that way. I kept an image of the powder-blue sky, the cumulus clouds, the brambles, saplings, and trees—all imperceptibly transforming from winter's dormancy to spring's vibrancy. And with eyes closed, I heard songbirds reclaiming their tunes and breezes whispering of warmer days to come. After an unmeasured time, a soundless signal caused our eyes to open together.

As if being in mid-thought, the Judge said, "'Either the darkness alters or something in the sight adjusts itself.'" He looked at me, and now he sat completely in shadow. "Which is it, AJ?"

I had no idea what he was asking and told him I didn't know the answer.

"I suspect no one does. But I know I *must* build that cradle. Time is limited, and my plan calls for the cradle's completion and for my leaving behind a letter in a sealed envelope. Soon. It must be soon. I'll write his name on the envelope and place it on the kitchen table. But first, I must finish that cradle."

"Can I help?"

"Yes, but not now. I'm done for today. Tell you what, could you help me glue a few pieces together next week?"

"I'd like that."

"In the meantime, you need four packets to meet your goal. I'll make the purchase." He searched his jeans and found the exact change. "Let's put these packs in the shed, and when you come by again, we'll figure out where to plant the seeds. Who knows, maybe you and I will rough out a flower bed? I'm not opposed to impractical beauty." He winked. "All right?"

"Sure."

"Good. Now, young fella, if you'll take these drinking glasses back to the kitchen, I would be obliged. I couldn't carry both without losing my balance, and making two trips would be embarrassing."

I grabbed the glasses and poured the remains onto the dormant grass. Before leaving, I looked back and saw a man I should have recognized.

***

After school on Tuesday, April 23, my friend Bobby and I walked to his house. He invited me to play catch because his father had bought him a new baseball glove, and Bobby wanted to break it in. I used his old one. On Monday it had rained all day but on Tuesday the sun was out, and while standing in Bobby's backyard that faced south, the earth breathed a fertile fragrance that mingled last year's decay with this year's growth.

We stood about thirty yards apart and threw a baseball, simulating its movements on the field: zipping like line drives or floating like pop-ups or hopping over grass like grounders. We played until our arms ached, which didn't take long, being inactive for months. Then we sat awhile on his back porch, and his mother came out and gave us Cokes and a bowl of pretzels. She was a pretty woman with short brown hair and an athletic body, wearing a blouse and skirt that probably came from Macy's. She smiled easily and spoke softly.

Alone, Bobby and I talked about school and teachers, about baseball and girls. Then we played catch again. I felt alive. The spring air, the soft ground, the budding flowers, trees, and bushes; the perfection of a cowhide sphere with bright red stitches whirling between us, forever proclaiming a fresh beginning.

Time got away from me, and when Bobby's mother mentioned her husband would be home soon, I returned his old baseball mitt and walked a fast pace home.

I was not surprised to see my father's truck in our driveway, but as I came closer my feet seemed to miss the ground, my stomach sank, and the hair on the back of my neck stiffened. How is it that a person knows when something is terribly wrong? How is it that knowledge, apart from his natural senses, seeps inside a person? I opened the side door that led to our kitchen. Inside, everything was as still and soundless as a forsaken church. I was afraid to touch anything.

I moved to the living room and found my father sitting in his club chair. He stared toward the picture window. On the end table next to him stood a bottle of whiskey. He rarely drank hard liquor, but now he held a half-empty glass of it.

"Dad?"

I called twice before he turned his head, and it took a moment before he seemed to recognize me.

"Your mother is gone," he said in a dull voice. "She left us." He held up the tumbler, looked at it, and drank the remains. Then he refilled the glass.

His words hit hard. I knew exactly what he had said, but I didn't want to believe it. "Where did she go?"

"I don't know."

"When will she be back?"

"Never."

My knees buckled. I almost fell over but caught myself.

"Can we we look for her?"

"No."

I was drained and afraid, but more than anything I was angry. He sat there drinking, doing nothing. Over time, it was a familiar sight. But on that day, I couldn't stand there another minute without exploding. I walked to the front door and held the knob when a final thought came to me. "Did she leave a note?" I thought she must have left a message for me—one of hope, regret, or even love.

He took a hard swallow of whiskey and looked straight ahead. "No." And his voice cracked.

I walked outside. The sun was almost down and spring's warmth had turned back to winter's chill, spreading over houses, streets, and land. The flag on our mailbox had been up that morning; now it was down. I looked inside the metal box and along with the mail was a package from the US Seed Company. I took it and left the rest behind.

Standing on the edge of our property with the deepening cold and darkness, I thought of all the people I had visited while selling seeds. I wondered who, of all those people, could I turn to? Who would take me in?

NINE

2022

After seeing Mr. Kenton for the last time, I checked out of the motel, left town, and headed for home. With me, I took his final story and the two envelopes that held his parents' letters, which he had taped closed. As he handed me the envelopes, he said, "It's up to you."

Earlier that day while we sat on wrought-iron chairs, the April afternoon turned chilly. I slipped on a windbreaker; he pulled a wool jacket over his denim shirt. As we huddled against the sudden cold, he explained that after a series of growth spurts—as many boys experience—by the age of sixteen he could pass for eighteen, so he dropped out of school and traveled west. He revealed how, after his mother died, his father's drinking increased. Many nights the man couldn't sleep, so he prowled through the house and sometimes wandered outside and stood like a statue for an hour. Mr. Kenton never felt at ease in that house.

Out West he changed his name and snagged his first job at a Gas 'N Go where he performed every menial task given to him. After two years of that, he landed a job with the National Forest Service that allowed him to see much of Idaho.

"I would have stayed," he said, "but my father's death called me back. Ironic, isn't it? A man who never smoked cigarettes contracted lung cancer. It probably ties to that damned factory where he worked all those years."

When he finally returned, an envelope with his name lay on the kitchen table. Before opening it, he rummaged through a certain drawer and found another envelope, one he knew was there, an older one he had always feared to open until that day.

"Those letters altered everything. I saw things overlooked before like the way my mother dressed, her arms and legs always covered. Indeed, a great light broke upon me."

Soon after reading the letters, he began his first book. He told me it was plain luck that during his nine year absence, Susanna Billings had made a small splash as an artist, selling some paintings after making connections with a New York agent. He didn't know if her husband had anything to do with her success. But through her connections, AJ Kenton's career began.

"I stayed in my parents' house that first year. Then I sold the place and with that money and the income from my book sales, I bought Judge Franklin's place. It had been unoccupied for quite awhile, so it took a few years to restore it. Actually, I did very little updating, mostly repairs."

The buyers of his parents' home scrapped it off and replaced it with a modern, contemporary house with bold angles and abundant glass.

"After writing my eleventh book, I was finished," he said. "My books created a world which never existed, and I made a fortune from it. I never depicted the real world because I knew people didn't want it. I also knew of many harsh truths, knew they existed, and knew they would always exist. I didn't want to portray that world, so I created an idyllic one and turned my back on everything. I existed like Mrs. Warren without friendship or love or even touch. So, Jenny, with my books I often wonder if I gave people hope, or if I robbed them of hope. Did I make the right choice? I don't know. I suspect you pay a price either way. What do you think?"

That question, in one form or another, had been circling my thoughts since Mr. Kenton began his story. But the answer eluded me. In his books, people found ways to balance one another, they knew civility, neighbors helped each other; it was okay to do the right thing, love wasn't fluff but a foundation, it was good to hope for the future, and people may have stumbled but they righted themselves and walked straight again, or at least almost straight. If his books didn't show us who we are, didn't they show us who we should be?

"I think we'd better get you inside." I stood close to him. "Clouds are rolling in and it looks like rain."

"I suppose you're right. But one 'sad, last, gray hair': years ago the Kenton Town Council approached me and said with enough money they could refurbish the town and make it look the way people want it to look—the tourists—what they expect to see. Tourism, as you can surmise, keeps this town alive."

He stood and I gathered my notes. Like the first two afternoons, I overloaded my left side with my paraphernalia so that my right side could support the famous author-artist. I opened an arm to him. "Here."

"To help the town," he explained, "I set up a Trust so I can live comfortably, but the bulk of my income goes to the town's funds." He rested against me, feeling heavier today, allowing his full weight upon me. "I've kept my privacy, drifting farther away from everyone. I know now I should have been kinder to people. It wouldn't have taken much. But it's too late now."

As we moved toward the house, raindrops fell, the soft kind that serve as a friendly warning. "Do you think," I said quietly, "if you could do it all over, you would do things differently?"

He lifted his head from my shoulder and looked at me in a startled way but said nothing.

So, the interview ended and my dilemma began. Should I report the truth or bury it?

I tried driving straight home, but the rain came harder, and my wiper blades, although working like mad, couldn't clear the windshield. Besides, I was tired and hungry. And I was curious about those two envelopes lying on my passenger's seat, so I pulled off at an interchange with gas and food stops. For food, I chose McDonald's. Normally, I wouldn't, but a cheeseburger and a cup of coffee couldn't hurt, and inside the restaurant, I found a booth to myself. After a few bites and a gulp of coffee, I opened one envelope: the letter his mother had left for her husband years ago. Her handwriting was so jagged, the words were nearly illegible.

I'm leaving because I can't take anymore. I can't do this anymore. I'm empty. I have no feelings for you or for the boy. I want nothing. I ask nothing. Just let me go.

After reading it again, I thought how a person's life can twist in horrible directions. Then I opened the letter that Kenton's father had left him.

I hope you found what you were looking for, and I hope it's far from this house. I don't know how to explain things, but you should know that I wasn't always good to your mother. All I know is that sometimes things happen between two people in private, in the dark. Sometimes another side comes out. You find yourself doing things you thought you could never do. It's good you left when you did.

My stomach churned and after sliding the letter back into its envelope, I pushed it from me as if it carried disease.

I couldn't eat or drink, but I sat there a long time, wondering what I should do with those letters and with Kenton's final story. If I broke that story, it would build my career. More than that, as a journalist I had an obligation to write the truth. But I wondered if this particular truth would benefit anyone. What struck me most about his story was realizing how little has changed over the years. Society, people, problems. In fact, I wondered if things had become worse. Resentment and division. And then, somehow, a simple equation came to me: without change there's no hope, and without hope there's only darkness.

I looked up as a mother and daughter, who were leaving and emptying their trash, walked toward me. The mother looked to be in her late twenties, and the daughter appeared to be six or seven years old. The red-haired girl wore a white blouse, a green and blue tartan vest, and a navy skirt. She looked content with the world around her. She and her mother, I imagined, had stopped for a quick bite, and perhaps the mother had treated her daughter to dessert. The girl's innocent eyes briefly fell onto my worried face. Before they moved on, I noticed the girl hugged a tattered book to her chest, as if it were a favorite hand-me-down doll. Clearly, it was a treasure. I saw the title: *Accustomed to the Dark*, AJ Kenton's first published book.

I chose to stay inside until the rain stopped. Mother and daughter stepped outside, looked at the broken sky, looked at each other, and then laughed before dashing to their car. Doubtless they were undaunted by the rain that, to me, seemed like shards falling from a slate sky.

ACKNOWLEDGMENTS

Thanks to Jeff Blair, Yvonne de Sousa, Paul Eppard, and Brian Kurz.

ABOUT THE AUTHOR

Thomas DeConna was born and raised in New Jersey. He has poems and short stories published in a number of literary journals. His novel, *Season of Restorations*, has been critically acclaimed. Currently, he lives in Colorado with his wife Sheryl.

OTHER TITLES BY THOMAS DECONNA

THOMAS DeCONNA

NOTE FROM THOMAS DECONNA

Word-of-mouth is crucial for any author to succeed. If you enjoyed *Accustomed to the Dark*, please leave a review online—anywhere you are able. Even if it's just a sentence or two. It would make all the difference and would be very much appreciated.

Thanks!
Thomas DeConna

We hope you enjoyed reading this title from:

BLACK ROSE writing™

www.blackrosewriting.com

Subscribe to our mailing list – *The Rosevine* – and receive
FREE books, daily deals, and stay current with news about
upcoming releases and our hottest authors.
Scan the QR code below to sign up.

Already a subscriber? Please accept a sincere thank you for
being a fan of Black Rose Writing authors.

View other Black Rose Writing titles at
www.blackrosewriting.com/books and use promo
code
PRINT to receive a **20% discount** when purchasing.

9 781685 133153